THE ENO CLUB

THE ENO CLUB

GENE UPCHURCH

Firebrand Publishing publishes in a variety of print and electronic formats and by print-on-demand. For more information about Firebrand Publishing products, visit https://firebrandpublishing.com

ISBN: 978-1-941907-36-8 Paperback

ISBN: 978-1-941907-37-5 Hardcover

ISBN: 978-1-941907-38-2 ebook

Printed in the United States of America

*In memory of Pender and
all the good times in
Duke Forest*

Contents

Prologue

The old general rubbed his temples, the exhaustion of war causing a ceaseless ache behind his eyes. He could see the end of this sickening war through the dingy windows of James Bennitt's tiny farm house, where a handful of troops from both sides were gathering to witness the historic surrender.

He was weary, so weary, and filled with grief. It wasn't the personal grief of losing friends and colleagues in horrible and bloody ways, nor did he grieve for the time away from his family that he would never recover.

He grieved for the really good men, thousands of good ones with families and homes and futures and dreams, whose deaths came in ditches and fields across the southern part of this divided country. When he closed his eyes during sleepless nights, he knew their deaths came in awful ways, with musket balls that maimed but didn't kill instantly, leaving their targets to writhe in the dirt with no hope of help or salvation or anything to ease their relentless pain. They were in those ditches and fields because he told them to go there, and they went, and they died.

And now it was nearly over.

But he still had two problems.

Those whom he had vanquished on the battlefield continued to press for more concessions in the surrender document, creating a terrible conflict within the mind of the general who wanted to burn down the homes of his counterparts on the losing side. They were cowards in his mind who had betrayed their country and the constitution to which they had pledged the same allegiance as he when they studied together at the military academy. But his president wanted compassion, so he would agree to give them their horses and swords and a swift boot towards home if they would simply stop fighting.

Negotiating the end of a major war, however, was simple compared to his second problem which sat in front of him in one of farmer Bennitt's cane-bottom chairs.

The handsome leader of a barely known group of natives sat in that chair and stared at the weary general. The young Occoneechee had laid a package of papers on the dining table used as a desk by the general and waited.

These two men had met years earlier when the war was still young, and both sides could remember why they fought. On a spring day between battles as the general's army moved through the piedmont of the Carolinas, his soldiers encountered the Occoneechee huddled in a tiny enclave along a small, beautiful river that meandered and twisted through the area, often more a stream than an actual river, usually shallow enough to cross on foot without trouble. To call it a tribe was generous; the group was more like an extended family, and not at all like the violent and desperate Indians whom many of these soldiers would encounter in the coming years as the country expanded westward. These Indians were simple, peaceful folk who traded the skins of deer and beaver with local businessmen and had learned enough English to function in a new world.

They retreated to their enclave when they heard from traders that the whites who now ruled this land had begun a war with each other. This was not their war, not their fight.

But the general convinced them otherwise.

When his troops captured the Occoneechee and brought them to him, he could immediately see that their knowledge of the area and skills in the woods would help him since he was essentially an invader who had to rely on traitors, spies, scalawags and bad maps for the information to plan his strategies. Their refusal to help him melted away when he told them that they were, frankly, his prisoners. He also explained that this war was being fought by white people, but it was a war about black people and whether the country would continue to enslave them, and that brown people were just as likely to be enslaved as well if such a policy was not stamped out.

They had done their part, the general acknowledged. They were a peaceful people, but had done some things for him that his own commanders and soldiers couldn't, so he had concluded early on there was no reason for his army and general staff to know that many of the setbacks, ambushes, surprises, murders, kidnappings and thievery that hamstrung their enemy were handled by his unknown squadron, which had turned out to be clever, tireless, and brutal if necessary.

The papers on the desk were a treaty and a promise the general had made to the Occoneechee.

They already had their gold. The general delivered that when he got word that another surrender two weeks earlier at a court building a hundred twenty miles away had confirmed that the war was ending. The gold was delivered in canvas bags and loaded into a big chest, and he gave them the mule and a wagon needed to haul it away. He hoped it would be several days before they realized that half of those canvas bags actually held worthless metal coins confiscated from confederate warehouses. Those bags were on the bottom of the pile in the chest, just to be safe. He allowed himself a tiny grin at the thought of this trickery, which was the idea of a clever lieutenant on his staff, a ruse which got him promoted to captain on the spot.

Now, the general stared at the Indian's papers, the other part of the bargain.

"You know," he said to the Occoneechee, "only Congress can ratify a treaty."

The Indian stared back, unmoving in the uncomfortable wooden chair.

"You made a promise to my people," he said. "We did what you asked. Three of my family are dead because of it. You are the government, you are your people, you are the Congress here."

The general rubbed his temples some more. He was giving them land he couldn't give, making them a promise he feared his fractured government wouldn't keep, and creating an Indian nation that was completely illegitimate. There was no survey, no markings on trees or iron in the ground or kerchiefs on fence posts. There was only a handful of words on some flimsy parchment paper that loosely described a parcel of acreage a few miles from where they sat. The Indians had asked for a couple thousand acres, but these papers described maybe a thousand and the general knew the Indians couldn't tell the difference.

He already was being vilified by some in his government for being too generous, too lenient to those whom had been conquered. He was certain he would be criticized for this, as well.

One day, he thought to himself, *there will be war of a different kind because of what I'm about to do.*

But, he concluded, *that is a war for others to fight.*

He flipped through the treaty again without looking, signed it with a flourish, and handed it to the newly minted captain with instructions to send it to Washington with the surrender documents when those were finalized.

Then, he strode from the tiny farmhouse to end a war, his war.

Chapter One

The sound at the door was a whisper of a knock, more of a brush against the outside of the handsome door.

Reggie was on the phone with his wife, and the sound at the door distracted him. Even though he expected it, the sound caused his heart to pick up its pace and his mouth to moisten slightly. He didn't want to rush his wife because she might get suspicious, but what Reggie didn't know was that she was ready to hang up to return to the restless hands of her latest drop-in lover.

They finally said good night and love you and all that. As Reggie moved toward the door with high hopes, he reflected for a quick moment on his good fortune to be visiting a place that was unlike anything he'd ever seen, and he'd seen a lot.

He was tall and good at basketball, so he had made a nice career for himself in the National Basketball Association. He was a mid-level pro, a solid performer who enjoyed a non-stress role at the end of big games when the ball and the glory went to the big stars who made or missed the shots that win or lose championships.

One of his best buddies was a big star who flew in private jets and was surrounded by groupies and admirers and servants, and it was his buddy who had figured out this trip and invited Reggie and six other guys.

These eight guys were the only guests at a unique, nearly top-secret golf hangout. Thirty-six holes of perfectly manicured golf paradise on what used to be a Texas cattle farm, totally private, completely first class.

There was simply nothing like it anywhere.

Each guy had his own room and bath. No other guests were on the property – and that was a rule and a promise -- so they played as many holes as they wanted at whatever pace they wanted. They could play an eightsome and nobody cared because the place was theirs for three days.

Their chartered jet had landed at a small runway about a mile from the first tee. They were greeted efficiently and hustled to the golf course while their bags were delivered to their rooms. They were making bets, smoking stogies and talking shit fifteen minutes after wheels down.

Over the next three days, the boys would play forty plus holes a day, then collapse in the small but perfect little clubhouse for a magnificent meal that was prepared individually for each golfer.

The other meals were also unbelievable. Breakfast was hot and featured all the regular stuff to fill up a guy for a day of golf. Lunch was offered at the small clubhouse, but a quick call to the manager would result in lunch under a tent anywhere on the golf course. And, about every four holes, an exotic drink cart would be waiting with every imaginable refreshment and cigars. Reggie and the boys never saw the cart move, nor were they ever aware of how it got from one place to the next without being noticed, and they really didn't think about it.

But, enough about that, Reggie thought as he padded to the door in that graceful way of athletes who have supreme control of their movements. He grinned at the pleasure that waited outside his door.

He cracked open the door, and then opened it.

It was the ugliest hooker he'd ever seen.

Good lord, Reggie thought, *this has got to be a joke*.

He looked more carefully. He wasn't even sure this was a girl.

Whatever it was looked like an Indian, and poorly at that, and certainly not like the Indians on Saturday morning TV. He or she or whatever had an Adidas headband with bird feathers tucked into it, a big swag of wooden beads around the neck, and some war paint or badly applied makeup.

Reggie didn't know what to think.

After a few befuddled seconds, three large basketball players jumped from the darkness, laughing their asses off. Reggie was more relieved than startled, and his buddies shoved in his direction a real hooker who was a woman and good-looking and everything.

The Indian laughed also and melted into the darkness toward his maintenance shop, a fresh thousand-dollar wad of cash in his pocket for helping with the guest's little joke.

Reggie and his date retreated into his room where his experience was frustratingly brief and his performance embarrassingly amateurish. She shrugged and left.

As he lay there more or less satisfied, he thought about this entire experience and how wonderful it was.

He ran through his finances in his head, based on what he knew, which wasn't much because his agent and accountant controlled nearly everything. But he did the math the best he could and calculated that he could do it.

His basketball career would soon end, and

this is what he wanted to do with his money and his life.

He wanted to recreate this magical place back home.

If someone could do it on a Texas cattle farm, he could do it in a Carolina pine forest.

Chapter Two

The decades were unkind to the Occoneechee. Their claim to their land and their nation was constantly disputed over the years. The treaty and the grant of two thousand acres of Piedmont forest were more legend than fact, and the tribal leaders and their descendants were unable to provide any legitimate document that verified the price paid by the United States for their assistance during the war.

So, over the years, people took advantage of them. Hardscrabble farmers poached little tracts here and there on the edges. Some of the early farm houses were burned, but the Occoneechee were uncomfortable with this violence and worried that retaliation from the whites would be disastrous.

They eventually took a different approach. When a squatter tried to claim a piece of tribal land, the Occoneechee began to offer them a lease that would expire when the current farmer or his descendants no longer lived on the property. Farmers eagerly accepted these terms, especially since the tribe required no payment. As a result, a handful of simple farms and remnants of farms dotted the reservation.

The few remaining Occoneechee lived in small shotgun houses and rotting mobile homes on the edge of their land and at the end of a rarely maintained gravel and dirt road dotted with axle-cracking pot holes. They lived in abject poverty; only a few had jobs, and none had hope.

The road was called Indian Road by the locals, even though it didn't show up on any maps and was more path than road. Indian Road came off the main state road, and an "S" curve about fifty yards in blocked the view of the ramshackle village from people driving the main road. Before the curve, there was a state sign that said, "No outlet," with a smaller sign below it on the same post that read, "State maintenance ends here." Anyone who continued driving past the signs and the "S" curve found themselves amidst a cluster of unpainted wooden shacks with rusting metal roofs, several mobile homes that were falling apart, pink insulation dangling underneath them, and an upholstered chair on the porch if there was a porch. There also were the remnants of a burnt-out house at the end of a gravel driveway, with a small travel trailer parked next to it.

Next to that house was the largest house, though by no means luxurious or nice or even livable by most standards. It was the home of the tribe's leader, Jezz, a large and imposing woman with a head of tumbled and wild gray, red and black hair. Feathers poked out of that tumbled mess which she said were eagle feathers but everyone knew were those of a lowly hawk. Her neck was ringed with a collection of turquoise jewelry, and she dipped snuff all the time. She was a spectacular sight.

Jezz was the chief, which is what everyone called her because no one knew what to call a female chief of an Indian tribe. She was still a teenager when she became chief after her father died. She was the natural heir to the role, and nobody else wanted to do it.

Like their tribal land, Jezz's blood had been infiltrated over the generations by whites and an occasional black. She was about a quarter Occoneechee, which made her more genuine than nearly anyone in the tribe, and it made her their leader.

Early in her rein, the local county commission was briefly overtaken by magnanimous liberals who were anxious to make their county a shining beacon of equity and racial diversity and focused mainly on efforts to give the large black population more opportunity in the community and more say in how it was run.

During this time of glorious enlightenment, one of the liberal commissioners was on a hike through the forest, doing what liberals do, admiring the flora and fauna and all that was around him until he got lost and disoriented and eventually emerged into the tribe's pitiful

little enclave. He was relieved to find civiliza-
tion, but unsure of what he'd found or where
he was because, like most everyone, he had no
idea this road or these people existed.

As he wandered about the desperate little
community, Jezz emerged from her home and
approached him. She was magnificent, tall and
lean and dark with crazy hair and feathers, and
the liberal county commissioner was transfixed
by her looks. She invited him to her front
porch, brought him iced tea, and they sat on
the steps of the porch where he learned who
these people were.

Jezz told him the story of the promise to
her people made at the end of the Civil War by
a great general. He listened for an hour as she
told him how, years ago, the university wanted
to expand its research forest to include the
tribal land. The lack of deeds and proper
records made this especially difficult, but the
attorneys finally reached an agreement with
Jezz's father that allowed the Indians to continue to live on their so-called land, even
though they couldn't prove anything, and allow
the university to train its forestry students and

study the trees and flora. The university paid the tribe a tiny honorarium to keep it quiet. It was a good deal for all; the tribe had some income, which all went to Jezz's father and then to her when he died, and the university had the inside track on a priceless asset when growth in the area and the need for neighborhoods and subdivisions pushed toward the forest.

Jezz became emotional as she continued her story, tears of frustration boiling in her wonderful brown eyes, and described the little tribe's frustration when they would hear about that other tribe in the far western part of the state's mountains and the stories of skyscraper gambling casinos and great wealth coming to the people who could prove their native Indian lineage. She said her people could never understand why one tribe of native Indians could enjoy such splendor and others could suffer like this. She said this all whilst dramatically waving her hand towards the mess on Indian Road.

When Jezz ran out of story to tell and wiped her tears, the liberal politician delighted in what he heard and marveled at the prospect of helping these people of color also, because their plight was as desperate as those of the blacks in the community.

As soon as he could get it scheduled, the liberal do-gooder added an item to the agenda of the county commission's meeting dealing with an "issue of people of color," and on the day of the meeting, fetched Jezz from her sad little home. He coaxed her into wearing a dramatic Indian headdress like in the movies. She had strongly objected to this idea, because her wild hair and bird feathers were her statement look, and she admitted that neither she nor anyone in their tribe had such a headdress. But he found one in the costume shop of the local community theater and embellished it himself with feathers and beads and other things that he thought would add drama to her appearance.

Which it did.

The community had no idea that Indians were in their midst until the spectacle at the county commission meeting, where the liberal politician described their plight and the injustice that had been done to them. The local newspaper reporter showed up for what was going to be a boring meeting but got a page 1A story with a photo when the beautiful Indian chief in full regalia spoke to the commission about her tribe's story and the challenges of being an Indian in today's world. That led to a front-page Sunday edition story in a few weeks with more details and photos of the pitiful little community at the end of Indian Road.

It was dramatic for a brief moment but, at the end of the day, it meant hardly anything.

The commission's only action at its meeting was to recognize the tribe as a "sovereign entity" which was not a legal term and meant nothing but made the liberals feel better. The liberals had breathlessly wanted to bestow upon the tribe the honor of being a "sovereign nation," but the county's lawyer warned that they lacked the authority to declare such a thing and besides what would happen if one of the black neighborhoods wanted to be a sovereign nation also. That was the end of that.

Naturally, the liberals were drummed out in the next election by the local white establishment who couldn't get their brains around sharing power, the economy, a seat on the bus, or anything else with someone who didn't look like them, even if they wore a spectacular headdress and had been persecuted and abused for multiple generations.

Jezz, meanwhile, returned to her home on Indian Road and threw the headdress onto a pile of rotting trash in her back yard.

Chapter Three

Jezz's father had steadfastly refused to negotiate on one point when he and the university people were splitting hairs about the forest.

He insisted that one of his people always had to be in charge of the forest, a person his people trusted to uphold the needs of the tribe.

The university finally conceded, and that person now was Jim. He had inherited the role of chief of the tiny tribe and forest manager from his mother, Jezz, who was happy to step aside and watch TV in her miserable home.

This was a dream job. He was outdoors all

day and completely in charge of what he did and how he did it. He'd done it for 10 years now, so it was easy. Jim kept the fire roads clear and made sure the gates at the public roads weren't blocked.

Even though the forest was technically private, the public could use it for hiking, biking, picnicking or screwing. If the university needed to keep folks away from an experiment, Jim would arrange for a fence to be built. Most of the experiments didn't need a fence; the pointyheads from the university would plant some trees or other plants, watch them grow over several years and measure them and take samples and stare at them. Occasionally, they would clear cut a section of the forest and re-plant it for experiments that would take decades before there were any results.

Mainly, Jim prowled the forest to make sure he knew everything that was going on. He was always frustrated to find shotgun shells or the gutted and rotting carcass of a deer or the re-mains of a campfire. None of those were al-lowed, yet it was rare for Jim to catch anyone.

The forest was truly beautiful. The home

sites of the original white farmers had been abandoned and reclaimed by nature, with the overgrowth providing a haunting, soft outline of simple homes and lives that had come and gone. A major part of its beauty was the New Hope Creek, which cut through the middle of Jim's forest and, over the eons, had carved spectacular valleys and cliffs that were very unusual for this flat part of the state. The bluffs were very popular for picnickers and horny college students, and Jim didn't care about any of that unless they set fire to something. The creek softly drained into the Eno River and eventually trickled by the comfortable enclave where an army found and captured Jim's ancestors.

Today, he parked and locked his truck and slowly wound his way into the deepest part of the forest, a heavily wooded area of hardwoods and thick underbrush. He'd been here many, many times.

It was a frustrating and slow walk, with lots of underbrush and briers and old muscadine vines to push out of the way. The heavy canopy of the century-old hardwoods blocked the midday sun and gave the forest a twilight feel. Rotting leaves and debris made the forest floor feel like a waterbed, so it was a tough walk.

He zigged and zagged through the tangled underbrush, but his internal compass helped him move in the same general direction.

The black body bag draped over his right shoulder was not as heavy as some of the others, so today's walk wasn't so bad. Some were so heavy he had to drag them. He stopped and rested for a moment and shifted the bag to his left shoulder before resuming his hike.

When he arrived at the abandoned well, he dropped the body bag on the ground and pulled back the tree branches and other forest debris that disguised the piece of rusty chain link fence that covered the opening to the well. He had used a similar design on other old wells in his forest to keep dogs and people from falling into them, but this is the only one he disguised.

After he wrestled the fence away from the opening, he reached for the body bag and gave it a tug toward the hole. This bag was lighter than most. *It must be a kid, or a woman,* he thought as he yanked at the rubber bag. As he did, the loose dirt under his foot around the hole's opening collapsed. He churned furiously, but more dirt gave way, tumbling into the hole. He grabbed for whatever he could, but there was nothing. Then he fell, grabbing at air, his head and arms brushing sharp rocks as he fell into the darkness.

His arrival at the bottom of the well was cushioned by the other body bags he had dumped here. Still, he was stunned and maybe unconscious for a minute or two, perhaps from his head hitting some rocks on the way down, but he couldn't believe what had happened. He sat there for a few minutes while his eyes adjusted to the total darkness and while his brain adjusted to his dilemma.

He didn't have a flashlight, of course. He felt on his waist for his smartphone, and it was there. He switched it on. No bars. No cell service. Of course. He was in a deep hole. But it had a flashlight! Now he wished he'd charged it last night. Sixty-five percent battery power.

He used the little light to look around. It

was a scene from hell. Black body bags, perhaps twenty of them, in a heap. He wondered why there was no stench from rotting human flesh, and he supposed that the body bags were doing their jobs. It was dank, but no standing water.

He looked up. The sky was a dime-sized hole straight above. Everything else was dark.

He tried to calm his racing heart and checked himself for injuries. He was sore, and his head hurt, but he appeared to be okay.

Now what?

He wondered how long it would take for someone to notice he was missing. He lived and worked so independently and freely that it might be days and days before someone at the university thought about him. A hiker might find his truck, but that would raise no suspicions.

His best option was to climb out of this hole and tell no one what happened.

If he was rescued, he probably could explain his way out of this mess. He knew most of the local sheriff deputies because they helped him deal with trespassers, and they probably would believe that he was working in his forest when he found a body bag, an abandoned well, and fell in when he looked down the shaft.

The drug dealers were another story.

Chapter Four

He surprised them one winter afternoon at the edge of the reservation, digging a shallow grave for one of their victims. They were local thugs and immediately surrounded him, large pistols pointed at his head, and forced him to his knees, head bowed, ready for execution. But they finally agreed his unexplained disappearance would bring a bunch of cops to the forest where they might discover some things, such as dead bodies, which was not good for their business.

So, they made him an offer.

Two grand per body. Any time they needed to dispose of someone, they would text him a secret code and meet him at a drop spot. They didn't care what he did with the bodies as long it was permanent and never discovered. One of them shoved the barrel of a large pistol in his right nostril and promised him that their bosses from Philly would deal with him if anyone found out.

Now, deep in the well, he wondered if he would die here, undiscovered. Or if he would die if the cops rescued him and the Philly drug lords didn't like their victims being discovered.

He stared at the hole in the darkness above and thought that the hopelessness of this situation was as hopeless as his arrangement with the drug dealers.

He tried to escape the drug dealer's world after his fourth body. He told them he'd do one more, and then no more.

They glared at him, and then at each other.

Jim's eyes suddenly were on fire. He couldn't see, and he flailed helplessly as he got tackled to the ground, another dose of pepper spray in the eyes and up the nose. Jim gagged and thrashed, but his hands were quickly tied behind him and a black bag pulled over his head. Jim's eyes were killing him; they hurt so bad he wanted to gouge them out, except his hands were bound behind his back.

"So, you want out?" asked a tough voice.

Jim was so scared he nearly wet himself.

"You think you want out," the tough voice growled. "You've seen us, and you know too much."

The black hood was pulled from his head, but Jim was disoriented and nearly blind, so he couldn't really see anything but three fuzzy figures huddled over him.

The fuzzy figures drove him to his little house and dumped him in his living room, hands still tied behind his back. One of them grabbed Jim's commemorative Atlanta Braves baseball bat from its rack on the wall and swung it at the back of his head. It felt like his eyes had been knocked out of his head, then darkness.

Jim didn't remember building a fire in his fireplace. He didn't have a fireplace. What's all this fire? Jim's head hurt so bad he wanted to vomit, and his eyes burned. As he started to regain his senses, he saw flames and smelled gasoline. *My house is on fire!*

He was in his own living room but couldn't figure out how to get out. His hands were still tied behind his back. He spotted the big front window, lowered his shoulder and smashed his way out of the burning house, tumbling awkwardly into the boxwoods under the front window.

He scrabbled away into the middle of his front yard and watched his house burn to the ground. The fire department arrived in about ten minutes but couldn't do anything, especially after the propane tank exploded. They snipped the plastic wrist bands and called the cops, who bought the story that his house was torched during a robbery.

Jim sat on his lawn, mourning the loss of his house and watching the firemen and gawkers point at the smoldering ruin. Neighbors came to express their dismay.

A tough voice suddenly was in his ear.

Now, are you in? Or not?

So, he was in. He had no choice.

Now he was in this dank well with twenty bodies.

He spent a couple of hours trying to climb out, but the walls were too vertical and damp with moisture, and there was nothing good to grab on to. He might get up ten or twenty feet, then he'd grab a loose, wet rock and tumble back to the cushioned bottom of the well.

He lay back and rested, conserving his strength, and began to realize that food and water would soon become an issue. And light. His little phone now had five percent power. The dime-sized sky above him had faded. Nightfall was approaching.

The dime came and went twice before hikers found the body bag. Suddenly, bright lights shined on him, and his deputy buddies yelled for him that they'd get some rescuers to haul him out.

Chapter Five

The discovery of the abandoned well filled with dead bodies was a sensation on the local news. Jim was interviewed by breathless TV reporters about his dramatic discovery of a body bag near an open well, and tumbling in, and spending several days awaiting rescue amidst rotting corpses. He was the darling of local TV for a couple of days. He left out the part about how all those bodies got there.

There was no return to a normal life for Jim. There was silence from the drug lords, and he didn't know if they would return to their little routine with him, or whether they had made other disposal plans, or were planning an ambush to silence him.

He suffered several weeks of strangling anxiety and paranoia and fear of sudden death, so he was actually relieved to hear from them when his phone buzzed. The secret code, tomorrow, the usual place.

He was strangely unafraid.

At least something was happening.

The usual place was an abandoned sewer lift station, situated on several acres donated to the county by the university. The tribe had protested the university's authority to donate the land but had been ignored. The lift station had its own access road, a half-mile of crooked and unmaintained rocks and dirt. Sewage flows downhill, so the lift station was in a small natural valley, now covered with vines and honeysuckle and kudzu.

Jim hiked in from several miles away, cutting through the forest and arriving at the lift station two hours before the appointed hour. He chose the highest point on a hillside overlooking the lift station and lay on his stomach in some thick brush and watched through binoculars. He wore his camos, and he was certain he wouldn't be spotted.

A sniper rifle was by his side.

He lay patiently, listening to the sounds of the woods around the old lift station, the birds and the bugs all adding their voices to the quiet, natural symphony that made working in his forest so wonderful. But dumping bodies down a well had stripped the wonder from his life and his job, and something needed to happen. It would end today.

A dirty white Suburban surprised him as it slowly inched its way into the sewer station's little clearing in the forest. Jim stared at it with alarm. The druggies usually showed up in an old low-rider Cadillac, so something wasn't right.

The Suburban paused for a minute and then backed up in the direction of Jim's hiding spot and parked. Jim stared through his binoculars. Pennsylvania plates. Could these be the Philly bosses?

As he tried to make sense of this, the front doors of the Suburban opened, and strangers emerged, white guys, not the usual black druggies. They looked around cautiously, professionally. A third guy emerged from the back seat, opened the tailgate, and handed out assault weapons. The driver issued some instructions and pointed in several directions around the lift station.

Jim watched carefully as the three guys spread out, one of them in bushes near the Suburban, another behind a brick wall on top of the lift station's big tank, and another in a ditch. They had perfectly triangulated the spot where the dirt road entered the lift station's clearing.

An ambush.

Jim waited. And they waited.

Were they waiting for him?

Soon, Jim heard the soft crunch of big tires on gravel, and the old Cadillac slowly entered the lift station clearing, the thump-thump of loud rap pulsing in the car. The car stopped abruptly, probably when the driver spotted a dirty white Suburban instead of Jim's blue truck. As soon as the car stopped, Jim watched in astonishment as the Philly guys suddenly emerged from hiding and raked the Cadillac with automatic weapons from three sides. The old car rocked back and forth as bullets blew out the windows, blowing gaping holes into the fenders and the tires exploded. Jim could see the horror inside the car; the three occupants flailed around as bullets knocked them back and forth, then they were out of view. After a few seconds, silence. The Cadillac oozed smoke and dust, and there was a pathetic wheezing where a bullet had punctured something in the engine, but there was no movement from inside.

The Philly guy in the ditch slowly walked to the car, emptied his weapon into the passenger compartment, and joined his colleagues as they walked toward the Suburban.

Jim wanted his life back, and now was his chance.

He put his crosshairs on the head of the driver and slowly pulled the trigger. The round missed, but blew apart the driver's throat, and he fell to the gravel, writhing and clutching at a throat that was gone.

Jim quickly chambered another round and

fired at the guy from the ditch, catching him in the shoulder, spinning him in a circle. The third guy frantically looked around and tried to hide, but couldn't tell where the assault came from. His hiding spot was perfect for Jim, who dropped him with a round that passed through his heart and spine before smashing into the Suburban's fender.

The ditch killer tried to get up, clutching his bloody shoulder, looking for his dropped weapon. He was on his knees. Jim took careful aim and then it was over.

Jim lay very still.

He waited a minute or two in case stragglers or other ambushers lurked, then quickly got up from his hiding spot and scrambled into the clearing. He heaved the rifle and leftover ammo into the gunky mess in the lift station's big open-air tank.

Surely someone would report the sounds of a gun battle in the woods, and deputies would arrive shortly.

But Jim didn't care.

He turned from the killing field and moved

toward the thicket surrounding the lift station, eager for the comfort of the forest.

Once through the thickest brush, he found a path and started to jog toward his truck, parked in a small ravine at the end of a horse path that was barely wide enough for it. He glanced over his shoulder as he cranked the truck, threw it into gear and roared down the horse path.

He was going way too fast for the narrow, crooked path.

Suddenly, his path was blocked. He jammed on the brakes.

He pumped the brakes, and then pumped them again frantically, but nothing happened.

He spun the wheel to avoid a collision. When he came to, he remembered two awful sounds, metal crunching and the sickening snap of a bone breaking.

Chapter Six

Rebecca and Charlie had loved each other for years and had come this way many times since she was a little girl. It was a Saturday afternoon tradition, a nice walk at a comfortable pace through the field behind the house, across the creek at the edge of the woods, and then into the trees on a well-worn path.

They both always knew where they were going and never deviated. It was the same every Saturday.

Rebecca wasn't sure how much longer

Charlie would make this walk, so she cherished the smell of the damp leaves and the sound of Charlie's iron shoes clacking on the occasional stone, and lovingly watched his head move up and down with his gait, his ears flicking back and forth as he heard sounds she didn't.

This was her one day of the week at the farm where she was raised and had vowed she would never return. Growing up there, she loved the land and its beauty, but hated the chores and the isolation and the notion she was a country bumpkin. None of her school friends teased her about being a bumpkin, because they too were bumpkins, but she could see from the magazines she read that there was a bigger world out there, and she was determined to escape the farm and be a part of it.

But she was back now every Saturday. She kept her vow through college and law school, but the death of her mom, the loneliness of her dad, her love of Charlie, and the softening edge of growing older brought her back to the familiar and comfortable farm. Every Friday night after work, she would drive the sixty miles from the state capital where she practiced environmental law back to the farm, have a snack with her dad, and then spend Saturday helping him pay his bills before saddling Charlie.

She wasn't married; she only had time for her dad and Charlie in her life. So, naturally, the dumbasses in the capital thought she was gay because she was moderately attractive but had no interest in them. Several of these geniuses had asked her out, and several others had harassed her, and she ended the career of another who said the wrong thing about what he'd like to do with her during an after-hours deposition that was being tape-recorded.

She wasn't always alone, however. It had become a Tuesday night tradition to stop at a little Italian place for chianti and pasta served at the bar by a bartender who happily followed her home and provided just what she needed, and nothing more.

Her focus today was on her time with Charlie and their easy walk through the familiar woods. Their trip was several miles, and the path carried them to the edge of their property. Sometimes they quietly crossed over into the university forest just to see something different, but not today.

As they walked, suddenly there was a gunshot in the distance. Charlie pricked his ears and broke his gait for a step or two. Rebecca wasn't worried; the nearby woods were full of hunters, so hearing gunshots was normal.

Then, all hell broke loose.

These aren't hunters, she realized. She was hearing a major gun battle, with the sharp sound of automatic weapons instead of the usual thud of hunter' shotguns.

She frantically yanked Charlie's head with the reins and touched his side with her heels. He eagerly broke into a trot, even a gallop briefly until he realized the age of his legs, and headed for home.

The gunfire had gone silent, and she slowed Charlie. He was exhausted and breathing heavy.

She heard a roar and couldn't get the sound to make sense. Charlie's ears pricked; he heard it also.

Before they could react, the horse path erupted in a noisy fury. Charlie jerked to a stop, his big eyes wide and head convulsing back and forth as he tried to turn to escape what he saw. Charlie tried to throw her, and she would've been in the ditch had she not been holding tightly to the saddle horn.

Chapter Seven

The university president sat in his opulent office, but he couldn't enjoy the view of the school's classic quad or its beautiful chapel or the elegant co-eds walking by in their little shorts, and he certainly wasn't thinking about the president of Chi Omega who had a key to his private entrance and stopped by twice a week to remind him why he loved being a university president.

Nothing was going right today.

They could handle the news of the body bags in the forest, and the university spokesperson – a former TV anchorwoman who also had a key to the private entrance – had eloquently explained over and over that the university obviously had no idea about illegal activity in the forest and would cooperate with authorities to find justice. Blah, blah.

What they couldn't handle were the nosy inquiries of a local newspaper reporter who was asking uncomfortable questions about the ownership of the forest. The reporter was exceptionally well-prepared and knowledgeable, which was rare in today's world of instant news and superficial and usually inaccurate reporting. But this reporter had a good source who made sure he knew everything.

The university president was dumbfounded when he read the reporter's first story that included an interview with a so-called Indian named Jim who said the property actually belonged to a tribe of Indians he'd never heard of.

Now, he sat at his enormous, polished conference table, crafted from an oak tree that had fallen during a storm in the university forest, and stared at a phalanx of lawyers, none of whom would look him in the eye but for vastly different reasons. First of all, none of them had the answer to his question and, second, one of them had privately resolved a nasty little situation when the DNA test on a cheerleader's surprise bundle of joy matched that of the president.

"What do you mean we may not own the forest?" the president asked the crowd in the room, hoping one of the legal geniuses had an answer.

No one said anything, until finally one of the lawyers cleared his throat.

"There may be a treaty," the lawyer said. "We don't know."

The president glared at him. He thought for a moment that it was odd that none of the lawyers around the table had been educated at the university's law school, and he didn't exactly know what that said about the law school.

The lawyer interrupted the president's thoughts and continued.

"The Occoneechee allege that they own the land by virtue of a treaty that was signed at the end of the Civil War," he said, looking down at the magnificent table. "No one can find such a treaty, and there's no record that Congress ever ratified anything like this."

"So, that's good, right?" asked the president.

"Well, no," said the lawyer. "There's an agreement."

He went on to explain the university's long-forgotten arrangement with the Occoneechee from the late 1950s in which the university essentially and technically acknowledged the tribe's ownership of the property and paid a small fee for lifetime rights to use the property for its forestry school.

The president sat at the head of the table, his mouth agape at this news.

"This mess gets messier," the lawyer said.

"The Occoneechee isn't even a real tribe," he said. "They aren't recognized by the federal government, so it's not like they could build a casino in those woods like some of the other Indian nations have done. So," he concluded, "we don't know who owns what, nor do we know who we negotiate with."

The lawyer continued with his pitiful update.

"They don't really have a chief," he said. "They have a so-called leader named Jim, whose mother was the chief or chieftess or whatever, and it's Jim who handles what little business they have and, if you can believe this, we actually pay him to be the superintendent of the forest.

"He could be a real pain in the ass and might go public."

The president had another meeting looming on his calendar, so he dismissed the lawyers with instructions to try harder and be more creative.

Now, he sat in his stately office and tried to figure out what to do next.

He had already announced plans to dissolve the forestry school, arguing that it no longer fit into a university that taught its students to think, not chop down trees, and to liquidate the forest, using the proceeds for various academic projects and provide much-needed funding for the school's endowment. He had carefully thought this through and was satisfied in his mind that it made total sense and would be broadly supported.

He was wrong. When he announced his plan, the campus responded with an uproar that startled him because he thought no one would really care.

But they did care. Protestors gathered outside his office, and they even launched a couple of eggs toward his windows. They burned him in effigy like he was some kind of third-world dictator or losing basketball coach and plastered posters on all the campus bulletin boards with his photo and a thick red diagonal line slashed across his face. Even worse, much worse, the protestors hung around for several days, spooking his Chi O paramour into staying away.

He thought he had his finger on the pulse of the campus but, as usual, had badly miscalculated. He was actually out of touch on nearly everything, so it surprised him that everyone loved the forest and thought it was a major asset to the university. He never went outdoors for anything, so he was clueless about how much students, faculty and employees all loved the forest and spent time there with their families, exploring the beauty, taking hikes, smoking dope and screwing in the bushes. It was a place anyone could go for free. Appointments were never necessary. The only rule was to show up and enjoy.

He sensed, and his staff confirmed, that there was sincere, serious opposition to his plan on a number of complicated fronts, including the threat to so many people who enjoyed it and the unknown but scary threats to one of the last remaining unspoiled natural areas in the region.

Those were difficult issues. But, as word spread about the hazy ownership and the claims of the Occoneechee became more public, the students and liberal academics on campus embraced the cause of the Native Americans as the ultimate reason to scuttle the president's grand plan.

It was a mess, but no one but him knew what a complete tangled up mess it really was.

He had a secret arrangement to sell the forest to a group of investors that included three of the university's most successful basketball players who had gone on to score unfathomable riches in the pros. They had big plans for the property, but he didn't know the specifics, and he didn't care. He just knew it was a big payday for the university and for him.

He had surreptitiously and carefully arranged several roadblocks for the hoopsters' project that melted when they agreed to pay a two-million-dollar cash fee to a broker/consultant owned by an obscure shell company. The payment was due up front, had been paid in cash, and the funds swiftly transferred to a bank in the Caymans which provided complete discretion but required funds to remain on deposit for at least two years, no exceptions. The players and their advisors would never peel back enough layers of the shell company to discover it was set up by the same lawyer who had adeptly extricated the president from his daddy duties in the cheerleader case, and who now quietly walked back into the office of the shell company's secret owner.

The Occoneechee leader had become the articulate and troubled face of the opposition to the president's plan and was being interviewed and celebrated by people who now professed great passion for the cause of a tribe they didn't know existed a week ago.

The president's instincts told him this plan was spiraling down the toilet.

"You know what we have to do," the president said to the lawyer.

"I will call Abel," the lawyer said.

Chapter Eight

It was a nearly full moon and cloudless night at the end of Indian Road, so Roscoe could see everything, including the hunched-over figure creeping along between the driveway and the bushes that lined the fence.

Roscoe's ears pricked up. Unlike his smaller, yappier brethren, Roscoe didn't rush out to greet his foe because he was better than that. He was a 95-pound shepherd mix, a veteran of police work. He was so smart and reliable that Jim didn't chain him or fence him, and he lived in a comfortable house next to the barn where he enjoyed plenty of blankets and water and food. His arrangement, actually, was better than Jim's, who was living in an old travel trailer parked next to his burned-out house, with a comical arrangement of water and sewer lines draped between the trailer and the house, duct tape holding it all together, sort of.

Roscoe lived with Jim because he retired early. He was highly trained to sniff drugs and, when commanded by a single, rarely-used word, would attack the flailing arms and legs of drug dealers and other criminals and wouldn't let go until commanded by another single word. In spite of his sophisticated training, Roscoe developed a preference for unauthorized yet joyful scrotum attacks on the miscreants he encountered, much to the giggling delight and chagrin of his handlers. Roscoe's favorite move was to grab an ankle or arm, shake it hard until the bad guy was on the ground, then take a hard chomp on his nut sack. It was hard to tell which Roscoe enjoyed more, the screams and shouts of a criminal with teeth in his penis or the stifled laughter of the deputies.

Anyway, a couple of bad guys got their disgusting lawyers to complain about Roscoe's tactics, and the ACLU heard about it and all of a sudden Roscoe was an issue for the sheriff's department. He made one more unapproved but highly effective groin move and went to live at the farm.

On this cloudless night, Roscoe watched. The figure moved toward the pickup truck and slid on his back under it.

Abel didn't know Jim had a dog, so he was focused on his task. It would be easy to cut the brake cable of the old truck, but that would only disable it in the driveway, and that wouldn't accomplish anything. The brakes needed to fail out on the open road, the first time Jim stepped on the pedal, hopefully at full speed in a sharp curve. A guy can only hope.

Roscoe silently padded over to the truck and stared at a pair of feet as Abel wiggled to get a better angle on his brake project.

Abel had just loosened a connection on the brake line and fluid started a slow drip onto the driveway when the big dog growled a guttural, menacing growl. Abel let out a brief scream, then hit his head on the truck's undercarriage.

"Easy boy, easy," Abel said as he slowly crabbed his way from under the truck.

Roscoe growled again, then started barking. And barking.

The floodlights on the house and barn came on, filling the yard with light as Abel ran down the driveway.

Roscoe held his ground, waiting.

Jim appeared on the front porch, loaded shotgun already at his shoulder. He took aim at the figure fleeing down his driveway and pulled both triggers.

Abel was already out of breath when the mixture of salt and bird shot burrowed into his left ass cheek. If his wallet had been in his left pocket, the damage wouldn't be so bad. But his wallet was at home.

Enough pellets and salt ripped into his ass that it caused his left leg to slip out of gear, and he hobbled down the driveway, looking over his shoulder as his butt started to scream in pain.

Then he heard Jim yell.

"Hunt!"

Roscoe hadn't heard that word in a long time, and it took a second before his instincts kicked in.

Then he was off, sprinting gleefully down the driveway. Abel was easier to catch than most of his victims. Abel put up his hand to protect himself, so Roscoe grabbed the outstretched arm and knocked him on his back. As Abel tried to scrabble backwards to escape the attack, Roscoe released the arm and deftly and expertly burrowed into Abel's groin. Abel tried kicking at the big dog, but Roscoe's teeth were locked in. The dog was having a great time.

Jim arrived at the scene and professed weakly and unconvincingly that he couldn't remember the release command.

The sheriff deputies burst out laughing when they arrived to haul the bleeding, miserable Abel to jail on a trespassing charge. Roscoe was happy to see them and finally let go of Abel's nuts when offered a delicious treat.

As Roscoe and Jim walked slowly back to the house, Roscoe stopped for a moment at the side of the truck and sniffed, but the fluid slowly dripping onto the gravel driveway was under the truck and out of sight, so they both walked on.

Chapter Nine

Rebecca panicked for a moment and looked around for others. Was she being attacked? Robbed? What was this truck doing on their path?

A quick glance, and she saw no one else. She could barely control Charlie, so she slid off his back and tied him securely to a tree.

The man in the truck was writhing in the front seat, slumped over toward the middle, his hand gripping the gear shift, and his face ashen from the pain. His leg was a mess, twisted unnaturally. Rebecca's first thought was the horror if this idiot had hit her and Charlie.

Rebecca had no patience with sick people, couldn't stand the sight of blood, and generally didn't care to help other people, but she knew she had to help this man.

She gingerly helped him out of the truck and into a more comfortable position, and he groaned, grimaced and gripped her arm tightly. She lay him on his back on the path, then evaluated the situation for a moment. She couldn't move or lift him and hoisting him up on poor old Charlie was a non-starter.

After a moment, she told him she was going for help and unhitched Charlie for the quick trot to the farmhouse.

She disappeared down the path, and Jim tried to gain his senses, his brain confused by pain. He may have passed out because it seemed like the agony briefly ceased. He could hear sirens in the distance and couldn't tell if the sheriff was coming to arrest him or rescuers were coming to save him.

But he knew he couldn't stay here, not here with his leg in a hole, the smell of fresh cordite on his hands, and a gaggle of dead gangsters a quarter mile away.

He tried to move his mangled leg, but the pain seared his brain and the sight of a piece of bone protruding from his shin made him retch and gag on a thimble full of watery vomit.

Suddenly, Jim was resting in a field of summer grass, a small stream trickling nearby, the sun glinting off the water, and the sound of crickets looking for each other in the pasture. The sun warmed his face, and he smiled, happy and comfortable for a change. He could hear a sound in the distance, like a small engine roaring, coming closer, spoiling his afternoon.

Jim was jolted back into consciousness, his pain raging more than ever. He looked over his shoulder for the sound and saw a John Deere Gator crawling down the path toward him.

Rebecca and her father were there with another man, a fellow Jim had seen around but didn't know. They lifted Jim into the rear of the Gator as he retched and held his head in pain, and then they were on their way to the farmhouse, the Gator lurching and growling down the uneven path.

They rounded a final curve before home,

and Rebecca almost missed seeing them. When she saw them, she touched her father's arm, and told him to stop.

There, in a straight line through the woods, was a series of stakes, white stakes with blue ribbons attached. This was something new. She stared at them and couldn't quite get her brain around what she was seeing and followed their progress from far away in the woods to the spot where her father stopped the Gator.

And there at their feet was a metal stake, driven all the way into the ground and painted florescent orange. A wooden stake was inches away, with some writing on it. She looked up and down the line of stakes and realized that they stopped either right at her father's property line, or were a little bit on his property.

Jim groaned in agony, reminding them that he needed attention.

The white stakes would have to wait, but Rebecca knew they were a threat.

Chapter Ten

She had no idea how much of a threat until her father called and said a lawyer was coming to visit. He wanted to talk about land and development.

Rebecca knew this day would come when somebody would want the farm for houses. The city was moving in their direction. She had always hoped her father wouldn't live to see it.

She wanted to be there, so she took a half day from work and drove to the farm, making sure she had time to surprise Charlie with his favorite treats. The horse was getting old also, and now she hoped neither her father nor Charlie would ever have to live somewhere but the farm.

The lawyer was what you'd expect: pin-striped suit and smelled like the Ralph Lauren counter at the department store.

He strode into the farmhouse, full of false friendliness and familiarity, a fake smile, and eyes that wouldn't look at theirs.

Rebecca had decided that she wouldn't reveal her professional credentials and perhaps surprise this guy during their conversation.

"The first thing we'll need to do," the lawyer said, "is for you fine folks to sign a confidentiality agreement. No big deal, just some paper to cover our bases."

"No," Rebecca said, just to knock him off his game.

"But, young lady," he said, "I'm gonna share some information with you today about some plans that are private, and my clients want it to remain that way. They're afraid that somebody's loose lips might stir up something that they don't want to deal with."

Rebecca glared at him. After a moment that was deliberately long enough to be uncomfortable, she then cited chapter and paragraph of several state statutes dealing with property rights and confidentiality and some other stuff that didn't really pertain but helped her make her point.

"Okay," said the lawyer, "are you his attorney or his daughter?"

"I'm both," she said. "We can either move on now, or you can leave."

The lawyer stared at her and, without speaking, moved to the dining room table where he spread out a large map.

Rebecca couldn't believe what she saw.

There, on their dining room table, was an incredible conceptual drawing. She got her bearings from spotting the local roads on the map and quickly saw that the heart of the drawing included the forest adjacent to their farm. She studied the drawing and could see what appeared to be the outline of golf holes, with little circles for proposed tees and greens, and straight lines connecting the two.

"What's this?" she asked, pointing to a long

narrow strip that ran down the entire west side of the map.

"Well, miss," the lawyer said dismissively, "that's reserved for utility easements."

She looked more closely and could see a large number 23 at one end of the narrow strip and a 5 at the other end.

"That's a runway. For airplanes," she said.

She ran her finger along the map from the large number 23 to her father's house. Two hundred yards.

She glared at the lawyer, who looked away.

Rebecca continued to study the map, and then saw the real reason for the lawyer's visit.

The conceptual design included what looked like a short golf hole − on their property! The hole began on one side of the small creek that ran behind Charlie's barn and ended on the other side. She looked closely at the design and saw that the architect even included a note to leave the big oak tree standing next to where the hole's green would be.

So, the concept included the university forest, plus about twenty-five acres of their farm.

"It'll be a beautiful spot," the lawyer said in

the voice of a preacher at a funeral. "And my clients, of course, will put up a fence and anything else you want. "I have a contract in my briefcase, if you want to talk particulars," he said. "We're offering a premium price per acre. I even have a check, if you're ready."

He stopped smiling when he saw the look on her face.

"Goodbye," she said.

As he gathered his map, he said, "There's more than one way to accomplish this."

"Don't threaten me," she said and pointed to the door.

Chapter Eleven

The map made no sense at all to Reggie.

He played a lot of basketball instead of going to class, so he never learned very much and never learned to think in the abstract or envision things that could be.

But even he could tell that this plan wasn't right.

"Whadya mean there's gonna be houses?" he asked, glaring at the man across the table. He then looked from side to side at his investment partners sitting on either side of him, his former teammates who had dipped deep into their retirement funds for this venture, for help. They remained silent.

"This isn't what we want," Reggie complained. "This is practically in the middle of town. There's no privacy. It doesn't look anything like that place in Texas."

The man across the table was John Lambeth, and he knew this would be a difficult meeting. Lambeth had made several fortunes as a med-mal attorney, and he was accustomed to getting his way. When he grew weary of suing insurance companies for his banged-up clients, he turned his passion for golf into a new business. He bought a failing country club; actually, he just bought the club's bank note, and for that piddling investment he got several hundred acres of excellent property, some decent maintenance equipment, and a clubhouse that would be something with a little work. He used his business acumen and aggressive style to focus expenses on what really mattered: getting the golf course in great shape and the clubhouse kitchen to fix a good meal. He also told the members to go to hell, it was his club.

He used the same business model to buy

five other troubled clubs and consolidated the purchase of food, fertilizer, fuel and grass seed so that his clubs were cost-effective, in great shape, and very attractive to golfers.

But, as he looked across the table at Reggie and the other so-called investors, he admitted the truth to himself.

He knew absolutely nothing about starting a golf course.

He knew how to buy them when they were in distress, but he was faking it with this project.

Reggie looked at his former teammates and could tell they shared his frustration. But they were dumber at business than he and had written some big checks just to get this far. They were just a few days from closing on the purchase of the property from the university but, before they could do that, they had to dig deep for another two million to pay some shady broker to make sure the deal went through.

"And now we get this?" Reggie asked. He was incredulous. No, he was pissed.

"The numbers simply don't work," Lambeth said as if he was explaining a crayon to a first grader. "Sure, we can pay the broker, buy the land, build the course and amenities and all that junk, but then we've got to operate the place. It might take years to become cash-flow positive."

Reggie looked at him as if he was speaking Chinese.

Lambeth tried to make Reggie and his boys feel like they had missed something or misunderstood, but he knew he had screwed up. When he developed the business plan that he pitched to Reggie and the other geniuses, he assumed a cash flow modeled on his other clubs, which created immediate equity when he bought them and already had decent cash flow from the members.

He knew this project needed the initial capital investment, plus three years of working capital in the bank, just to make it viable. But Reggie and his boys wanted it to be highly exclusive, so all the financials were messed up.

Lambeth wasn't about to put any of his own money into this thing, and he knew Reggie's team was tapped out on big money, so the only way to make it work was to sell some real estate in the new project, sell some memberships to some high-dollar guys, and hope it worked.

Reggie looked like he had smelled an old sock.

"This is bullshit," he told Lambeth. "Here we are just a few days from buying the land and you come to us with this bullshit. There's not even enough land. What if this farmer over here won't sell. You just gonna build seventeen holes? I thought we had plenty of land for thirty-six holes. That was the plan, wasn't it?"

Lambeth looked back at Reggie and tried to remain calm. He had directed the course designer and architect to use only about six hundred of the two thousand or so acres for the golf course, leaving plenty of acreage for an upscale housing village that was on a map that Reggie hadn't seen. There also was a real estate development company that Reggie didn't know about, but it needed capital before any dirt was moved.

The players had been pretty disengaged so far. They generally knew what they wanted, but the only thing they'd done besides write big checks was to have drinks with one of their buddies who was a **PR** guy and brainstorm names for their new venture. They went back and forth with some pretty stupid names until their buddy suggested The Eno Club, a nod to the small river that traversed the area and the namesake of the cross roads nearest the property. A couple of the tributaries that drained the forest trickled into the Eno, so it made sense to the players and was catchy enough to be cool. In exchange for his work, they promised the **PR** guy a free membership in their new venture.

Lambeth's phone buzzed, and he glanced at it. The closing attorney. He excused himself and stepped out of the conference room.

"What do you mean we can't close," he shrieked in a stage whisper into the phone. "I've got these guys lined up. What's the problem?"

He listened in disbelief. The seller doesn't own the property. We can't get clear title. A fucking Indian tribe may own it.

Lambeth clicked off, not sure of what to do next.

Chapter Twelve

The stench in the tiny trailer made her nauseous.

How can people live like this, Rebecca asked herself. *And what is that smell?* One source was probably laying at her feet, drooling on the floor, but even a clean Roscoe wouldn't clear this air. Jim's leg might be infected, but there was something rotten in here, probably in the tiny dorm fridge that Jim opened when he offered her a Dos Equis.

She declined the beer and began to explain the visit from the lawyer to her father's farm.

She and Jim had stayed in touch after the

accident on the horse path. They both knew that they would have to be allies in a big fight if that line of white stakes through the woods turned out to be what she was afraid they were.

She told Jim everything the lawyer had said and drew a rough map on a greasy paper grocery bag that was lying on the floor.

Jim couldn't get his head around this.

"And he said they'd bought the land?" Jim asked her.

"Not exactly," she replied, realizing that an important point like that hadn't even come up at the farmhouse. Next time, she'll ask more questions.

She continued. "All he did was show us the map and started to make an offer on part of our farm. We didn't get much further than that, and I didn't give him the chance to explain much else."

Jim slumped in his chair and stared at the dingy white cast on his mangled leg. He couldn't believe this was happening to his beloved forest, not to mention his nation's reservation.

He looked at Rebecca but didn't know where to start.

"They can't buy it," he said quietly. "They don't have the right."

"Sure they do," she shot back. "That's called a contract. A buyer and a seller agree on terms, and it's a deal."

"You don't understand," he said, raising his eyes to meet hers.

"What do you mean," she said.

"There's a treaty," Jim said.

Rebecca said nothing, waiting for Jim to explain.

Jim just stared at her, as if he was afraid to go on.

"There's a treaty, from the Civil War, and my people own that land," he said.

Rebecca had lived next to the forest all her life but had never heard of a treaty. She was vaguely aware that there was some sort of gentleman's agreement from decades ago that allowed the Occoneechee to live on the property, but she, like everyone else, always assumed that the university actually owned the property, used the forest as it saw fit, shared it with the tribe, and would toss them out when it got ready.

Jim slowly began to explain what he knew about the treaty, even though none of his people had ever seen it or knew where it was. All he knew was what had been passed down through the generations, and the stories were so specific that his ancestors had instilled in him a confidence that the treaty was real and could be enforced if ever needed.

"But I don't know where to start, so I never did," he said, slowing shaking his head.

Rebecca was intrigued and knew that this ghost of a treaty might be an opportunity to slow or stop the development of the forest and sidetrack the interest in the little parcel of her father's farm.

By now, Rebecca had forgotten the awful smell in the trailer and ignored the gargled snores and slurps of Roscoe at her feet.

"Tell me everything," she said.

And he did. He told her the stories he had been told about the conscription of his ancestors and how they had helped the Union Army as it moved through that part of the Carolinas.

Several were killed, but the tribe's work had been valuable as the federal government worked to quash the rebellion in the southern part of the new country. At the end of the war, their reward was the land.

"My people always said a powerful general put it in writing," Jim said, and then added sadly, "I wish I had it."

Rebecca thought for a minute.

"If it exists, I bet we can find it," she said.

Jim looked her in the eyes and sat up a little straighter.

"I also need to tell you about the gold."

Chapter Thirteen

Rebecca's father no longer had farm dogs to announce the arrival of guests and to harass and frighten anyone who approached the house and to bark and growl until he told them to stop unless the visitor was someone who needed to be barked at and growled at.

Even without noisy dogs to sound the alert, he knew someone was coming when he heard the car crunching down the gravel drive before he saw it; a big black Mercedes creeping and slithering toward his house like some terrifying creature on the hunt for prey.

He went out onto the front porch as the car stopped and brought his shotgun, which he leaned against the porch rail. It was unloaded, but the occupant of the black car didn't know that.

"Hello, Mr. Brown," shouted the lawyer as he stood up from the car, standing behind the open driver's door like a police officer during a traffic stop. It was the same lawyer who'd been there before. "May I speak to you?"

"Nope," Mr. Brown said.

"But Mr. Brown," the lawyer pleaded, still using the car for protection, "I have an excellent opportunity for you and your family, and I hope you will listen. Can I come closer and explain it to you?"

"Nope," was the answer again.

"But my client has assembled an excellent package for you, an offer to purchase your farm for forty percent above market," the lawyer shouted.

Mr. Brown picked up the shotgun and laid it on the top railing.

"Not interested," he shouted back.

"But Mr. Brown, please be reasonable,"

pleaded the lawyer, still shouting from the car. "We are willing to make a deal. If forty percent isn't enough, name your price!"

"Not interested, not for sale, and not talking unless Rebecca is here," Mr. Brown said. "We've already told you once, so get out of here."

The lawyer was getting frustrated and paused a moment to calm down.

"Mr. Brown, we have our ways," he shouted angrily. "If you're this hard-headed, we'll make life so miserable for you that you'll be glad to unload this place."

"Sir, we have our ways, too," Mr. Brown shouted back.

He picked up the shotgun, breeched it, pulled two shells from his pocket and slid them into their barrels, and snapped the gun shut with a noisy and theatrical flair.

"Out here in the country, we shoot tres-passers," he yelled at the lawyer, who crouched down behind the car door. "And you're tres-passing."

The boom of the shotgun startled the

lawyer, who heard the horrifying whiz of buckshot about three feet above his head.

"Get out of here!" Mr. Brown yelled, shouldering the shotgun, taking dead aim at the lawyer, who frantically jumped in the driver's seat, slammed the door, and cranked the big engine. Just as he threw the car into reverse and spun his rear wheels on the gravel, there was another boom, and the car shook as a load of buckshot shattered the right front headlight.

As the car sped down the driveway, Mr. Brown called his daughter and told her what had happened. She was secretly proud of her dad for turning away the lawyer, yet a tad concerned that he'd shot at him. Of course, the lawyer would be dead if Mr. Brown wanted him dead, and she knew the two shots were carefully chosen and expertly fired. Her bigger concern was the threats from the lawyer, and she had to take action. Now.

Chapter Fourteen

Rebecca sat in the so-called waiting room, a tangled mess of old magazines and faded furniture, and she could hear him doing his thing. Tom was on the phone laughing, talking loudly, telling a wild story, pacing and waving his arms around like a crazy person. As he hung up the phone, she heard him say, "See ya, Senator."

She had seen this guy at work, and he was the master.

Several years earlier, Rebecca was on the board of directors of a non-profit environmental advocacy group, and she tried to help them take on a well-connected gas company that wanted to build a pipeline through both a sensitive wetlands area and a pine forest that would disrupt or destroy the habitat of some woodpeckers. Rebecca helped her group develop a sophisticated strategy, with effective messaging to local and state elected officials and a mobilization effort of local citizens who loved the woodpeckers and thought they should be protected. They did it all: phone banks, mailers, speeches to the county commission and legislative committees, tours of the affected areas, all the things a group does to influence public opinion and change the direction of public policy.

It didn't matter.

They got steamrolled. A well-financed group called The Woodpecker Coalition popped up out of nowhere and completely confused everyone. The Coalition purported to be pro-environment, but its message was murky about the need to balance growth and economic development and we love birds and worms and snake darters, but we believe we need balance. Balance. They used that word to death. Balance. The Coalition got nearly everyone confused about who was advocating for the woodpeckers, and all the policy decision makers said they were for *balance*. That word again.

The only morsel tossed to Rebecca's group was a fifty-yard deviation in the path of the pipeline in the pine forest that saved a couple of woodpecker nests and shifted it into the property of a wealthy retiree who profited nicely from the tweak in the line. Beyond that, Rebecca's group got nothing, and Rebecca couldn't figure it out.

She learned much later that this Tom guy created The Woodpecker Coalition, a brilliant strategy to muck up the debate, confuse the issues, and give the elected officials a place to hide when they rolled over the true environmentalists. She also learned from a drunk county commissioner one night that nearly every elected official in the area had received a two-thousand-dollar campaign contribution from people who said they were board members of The Woodpecker Coalition. She did some light checking to see if someone had

broken the law, but nobody had reported anything so that idea was a dead end.

If this is how you play the game, Rebecca decided, *then that's what we'll do.*

She now wished she had worn a different
outfit to meet with Tom. As soon as she joined
him in his cluttered office, his eyes locked in on
the modest cleavage revealed by her silk but-
ton-down shirt, which had one button too
many unbuttoned.

"You know I love the university," Tom said.
"I've raised a lot of money myself and showed
them how to raise more. I've also cleaned up a
lot of messes and fixed a lot of problems."

Rebecca outlined the help needed by the
Occoneechee and how they needed their own
version of The Woodpecker Coalition to protect the land they were entitled to. As Tom
gazed at her neck or her chest or anything but
her eyes, she leaned forward and told him that,
without some professional help, the Occoneechee would lose what was rightfully
theirs.

Tom's gaze drifted to the top button of her
blouse, and he thought for a moment.

"Years ago," he said, leaning back in his tattered high-back chair, "the phone companies were desperate to keep the revenue from short-haul, long distance calls between a couple of nearby cities, while the business community and others wanted to eliminate the cost of long distance. The phone companies came to me because they were gonna lose the fight and look greedy doing it. So, I helped them create The Committee for Affordable Calling, or something like that. I had lots of friends who were preachers and activists in the black community, and we funneled thousands of dollars to their favorite causes and wrote speeches for them to give to regulators and elected officials, and made sure Christmas was memorable at their homes every year, if you know what I mean. The whole idea and message were that the phone rates of poor people would increase so rich people and businesses wouldn't have to pay for long-distance, and how's that fair?"

Tom grinned and wiggled in his chair with excitement.

"By the time that crowd of crazies got going, everybody was terrified to take on the issue, and it died on the vine. In fact, today you still pay for long distance between those cities. The Committee had so much fun and grew so strong that we eventually lost control of it, and they actually came back to haunt the phone companies and push them around years later. So, it was good while it lasted."

Tom burst out laughing as he remembered, and Rebecca smiled as she thought about how to make this work.

"The Occoneechee have no money, and can't pay you," Rebecca told Tom. "They may have some gold, but we don't know where it is."

The mention of the word "gold" moved Tom's eyes to hers, and then he suddenly became serious, almost so quickly that it startled her.

"You know I love the university," he said, glaring at her.

"The president," he said, "is a different matter."

"It'll be my pleasure to help you shove a hot pipe up his ass," Tom said, then stopped smiling for the first time.

"He raped my daughter."

Chapter Fifteen

The Maplewood Town Public Library was a shit hole. But at least it had windows and occasionally, some people. Leon was the head librarian in this shit hole, an ancient, smelly decaying building in a rural, decaying county where the largest business was opioid street sales to teenagers. Leon's library was the only sign of intelligence in a county filled with poverty and despair, where most kids didn't graduate from high school and those who did escaped and never returned.

He actually loved the library, with its musty smell and regular clientele of homeless and desperate characters who needed a place to escape the rain and lay their heads for a few moments of troubled sleep, even though the rules didn't allow it. Leon would only wake them when they snored or talked in their sleep and would only make them leave if they yelled at each other or pissed in the corner. Based on the stench of the place, he obviously didn't catch everyone who took a piss.

He knew he had to get out when he did some research and discovered that just as many books were stolen or missing or never returned as books that were legitimately checked out. During his lonely weekends, Leon would tour the county's yard sales and flea markets and use his own money to buy back the library books the thieves were selling for twenty-five or thirty cents each.

So, when he saw an online ad for a job at the National Archives, he saw a chance to chase what was left of his dreams to be a part of a collection that included the Bill of Rights and the Declaration of Independence. He would escape the hopelessness of his little public library and pointed a loaded U-Haul toward a world of significance.

Yet, today, his dream job was anything but, and it was dozens of miles from the nation's cherished documents. It was, instead, in the basement of a rural, windowless Virginia warehouse. The only sound was the swishing of the sophisticated climate control system that kept the temperature and humidity just right to preserve the thousands and thousands of boxes of the country's treasured history, and the only light were LEDs that switched on automatically when someone entered a particular area and triggered a sensor.

Leon's domain was the size of two acres, only the southwest corner of the enormous warehouse, and his job was to catalog the contents of thousands of dusty boxes. Sometimes, he would become so engrossed in reading the old papers and documents that the LEDs would assume nobody was there and shut off, so he'd have to stand up and wave his arm at the darkness to wake up the sensors. Day after day, he went through the boxes, rarely finding anything truly significant, but always finding

something interesting, and recording everything in a laptop in case anybody wanted to
know the location of something.

Hardly anybody did. Until today.

He'd never seen anyone like her, but he
worked in a warehouse basement and was from
Maplewood of all places, so that was under-
standable.

Rebecca was completely different from the
stuffy grad students or impatient authors who
occasionally, but rarely, found their way to his
basement. She smiled and was gracious and
kind as she asked if he had a few minutes.

"Absolutely," he answered, mesmerized by
his visitor whose scent was subtle but smelled
better than grime.

Her explanation and request took nearly
twenty minutes, but he was in no rush to return
to the dusty boxes of junk that his grateful nation entrusted to his care.

"So, you see," she said, "it's critical that we
find this treaty, wherever it may be. The future
of a Native American tribe may rest in your
hands."

Leon had never had this kind of conversation with an attractive woman, and he was more focused on her than on what she was saying, and certainly not focused on the warehouse's convoluted system for finding stuff.

Then, he remembered there was paperwork, always paperwork, before he could assist someone with their search through the country's junk box. He and Rebecca spent a few minutes filling it out, and he made copies of her identification and got her address and cell number, even though they were not requirements of the government, but just in case.

"When do you want to begin?" he asked, hoping the answer would be now.

"Now," she said, "if that's possible."

Leon began poking away at his computer, identifying the warehouse locations of Civil War papers. The computer told him there were twenty-seven thousand, four hundred and twelve locations of Civil War documents, in seven warehouses in five states.

Rebecca grimaced and slumped back in her chair. "Where do we even start?" she wondered out loud, looking Leon in the eyes.

Leon thought for a minute. He punched in

another query to his computer, this time asking the computer to look for treaties and miscellaneous documents, including correspondence between generals relating to the minutia of ending a war. After a minute, the machine told him where to find four thousand files, nearly all in his warehouse.

"Where do you want to begin?" Leon asked Rebecca.

She paused for a moment and contemplated the enormous, excruciatingly tedious task ahead of them, and thought back to the last time she felt so overwhelmed.

She was a brand-new young associate in a huge law firm, still dripping wet from law school and thrown into the middle of a massive lawsuit by her silk-suited senior partner who put her in charge of document production involving a twenty-million-dollar real estate dispute. She spent eighteen months reviewing one million documents, occasionally in tears from the frustration and the memories of grinding through the bar exam so she could sit in a windowless conference room for months looking at pieces of paper. When she couldn't even contemplate where to begin, she asked her boss where on earth to start.

"The first box," he replied, before heading to the country club for lunch.

"So," Leon said again, snapping her out of her brief reverie. "Where do we start?"

She thought for another moment, then looked Leon in the eyes.

"The first box," she said.

Chapter Sixteen

Four thousand boxes are a lot, Rebecca thought. After three days, she was exhausted and covered with grimy gunk. She and Leon had worked together and done maybe a hundred boxes, and he said he didn't mind helping because there were no standards or requirements for his work. He was largely unsupervised, and nobody complained as long as he was available to help people find what they needed.

They found lots of letters and reports on the sick, wounded, and dead, and the handwritten missives to heartbroken wives and mothers that their soldiers weren't returning. It appeared some were written but never sent or delivered, and Rebecca wondered sadly about the confusion and pain in those families.

But no treaty, or even anything like it.

Before they abandoned their search, they encountered a Civil War historian who was doing research on some arcane aspect of the war and was as frustrated as they were. He couldn't find anything, either. As they shared their frustration, he told them of an unknown collection of documents at Appomattox that he'd found useful. "It's not a secret," he said, "but they don't want people to know about it. You have to ask, and then get a park ranger to escort you to the basement of the old house that serves as the park service administrative offices. It might be worth it," he added. "It was for me."

And now she stood on a bleak, windy hill in rural Virginia, at the place where Lee surrendered to Grant. Lee's surrender was more famous, even though it preceded Johnston's surrender to Sherman a few weeks later in

Durham, the largest and final surrender of the war.

Rebecca felt strangely emotional as she surveyed the scattered little houses and buildings. Appomattox has not been preserved so much as recreated; hardly any of the structures were original because of fires and thieves and neglect, but it was still possible to imagine the tiny village where two great armies converged and waited while their generals figured out how to end a war. She was surprised by how she felt; she almost wanted to cry at the enormity of what happened here.

She took the tour and was surprised to learn that the house where the actual surrender took place was later dismantled by entrepreneurs who intended to rebuild it in Chicago as some sort of shrine.

She shook her head and wondered why no one fought to save that house in its original condition, and what would've happened if someone like her had fought for it as strongly as she is fighting for the forest and her family farm back home.

She wandered around the chilly village for

a while, trying to imagine two exhausted armies huddled among the trees and hillsides, ready to go home.

Rebecca walked to the park service office. The historian had told her to ask for the "Appomattox file room," which she did. Without speaking, a ranger in a smokey bear hat grabbed some keys and motioned for her to follow him to a non-descript doorway, which he unlocked and turned on a light. "Good luck," he said, pointing to the stairs leading to the basement. "Our archivist was let go last year because of budget cuts," he said, "so you're on your own."

She walked down a few steps and looked around. The basement looked and smelled like your grandmother's. She looked at some of the file cabinets and boxes and couldn't figure out any organization or system. So, she started with the files to her left and kept moving to her right, looking at every document, every piece of parchment, every item, a process that took three days. It was actually fascinating, and she found herself becoming distracted as she read the various documents that helped shape one of the most important times in the country's history.

When she emerged from the basement at the end of the third day, there was a message on her phone to call Leon.

"You won't believe this," he said.

Chapter Seventeen

Lambeth sat in the anteroom of the president's grandiose office, waiting his turn while the president finished a meeting.

In a moment, the door swung open and the president appeared, but no one stepped out to leave the meeting.

Lambeth was briefly confused, then saw the president's flushed face and rumpled tie and knew that his prior commitment had evaporated through another exit.

Lambeth brushed past the president, who turned and shut the door behind them.

"Goddammit," Lambeth said, "we've got to figure something out or these boys are gonna take a walk with their money."

No kidding, thought the president. *If this guy only knew there are two million reasons why I need this deal to close as soon as possible.*

They stared at each other like men do when neither have a clue about what to do next.

The phone on the desk buzzed, and the president said to send him in.

David Maynard walked in and shook hands with the president, who introduced him to Lambeth. After a few minutes of idiotic chatter about their golf games, they got down to business.

"So," Maynard said, leaning forward in his chair, "you need clear title to the university forest, and you don't have it and can't get it. Is that right?"

The president and Lambeth looked at each other, and then back at Maynard, and shook their heads yes.

Maynard stared at the president, and then

at Lambeth. Maynard had given millions to the university. He had secretly funded dozens of solutions when the university or its president got caught doing dirty deals, and he had generously ensured that cash was never an obstacle when the school was recruiting good football and basketball players. He had several shell businesses to fund these operations, but he didn't know that the president himself was in that business also.

Maynard had the best seats at the school's small basketball arena, and the president's box at the football stadium was named in honor of his father, who had created the state's largest title insurance company and handed it off to David when David turned thirty.

David took the company to the stratosphere with aggressive tactics that were verboten in the very conservative world of title insurance. One of his big hits had been to help a desperate developer in a rural county who had purchased land for a massive new neighborhood and discovered after the closing that the power company had an eighty-year-old easement right through the middle of it, even though no power lines were ever built. The developer was devastated because the title search hadn't revealed the easement, and the development that was going to propel his company to greatness was in peril.

Maynard devised a clever plan. The developer gave a piece of the action to the local state senator, who made the power company's lobbyist put in writing that they would never use the easement, and then he figured out how to put together a title search that would ensure that neither the developer or the title company would ever suffer.

That was thirty years ago, and Maynard had just left a meeting today with a room full of lawyers after the power company had notified the beleaguered homeowners who eventually bought homes from the developer that a power line was indeed coming through, and they were screwed. The lawyers had assured Maynard, the developer, and the state senator that they would be fine even though there would be troubled waters for a few days when the homeowners complained to the local TV station, but then it would soon evaporate from public view.

Now, Maynard stared back and forth at the two men sitting at the enormous hardwood conference table.

"I'll get your title," he said.

Chapter Eighteen

The wooden trunk arrived unsolicited and was delivered by two sullen state employees driving a seventeen-year-old state truck that wouldn't pass inspection if it was a private vehicle.

They lugged it to the front door of the Bennett Place, which was locked because legislative budget cuts limited staffing to two days a week, dropped it on the porch, and returned indifferently to their rusted vehicle, satisfied they had completed their delivery of a priceless piece of history.

It should've arrived at Bennett Place ten

days earlier, and perhaps even when the place was open for business, but the state mail system sent it to the Department of Culture Resources, where the bureaucrats x-rayed it for bombs and screened it for anthrax because such wasted effort added meaning to their lives. Then, they sent it by mistake to the Museum of History, where volunteers recognized that its intended destination was actually Bennett Place, and it sat on a loading dock for a week before it was loaded on an old truck for its final forty-five-mile journey.

The docent at Bennett Place knew nothing of the trunk's travails when she arrived for work in three days and found it blocking her path to the front door. After making some coffee and brushing away the dust and cobwebs from the nearly week-long closure required by the budget writers, she asked some school boys on a tour to take a minute from looking at their phones to help her drag the box into the old farmhouse, where it sat for four more days until her next day on duty, when she opened it. Inside, she found this letter:

Dear friends at Bennett Place,

We are the owners of the Cornwall Inn, located in a town called Cornwall-on-the-Hudson in New York. We are just a few miles from West Point, and for nearly two centuries our establishment has served travelers to this area and visitors to the military academy.

Our history includes a time when military officers stayed in our inn, and old diaries suggest they stayed here when the dormitories at West Point were full or they were on their way to a new assignment.

This trunk has been in our attic for many decades, and we believe it belonged to a US Army captain who stayed here after the Civil War and intended to return for his things but was killed fighting Indians out west.

We can't find his family, so we thought the Bennett Place should have his captain's jacket and some other personal items. Included in his letters is a bill from James Bennitt for damages to his house caused by the Army, so we believe he was there.

Yours in history,
Ingrid and Jim

The docent thought all this was mildly interesting, much more than the usual tour groups and trying to find somebody to cut the grass for free. She thought for a minute about what to do. She didn't really have a boss;

budget cuts had eliminated managers and supervisors and really anybody who got paid, so there was nobody for her to ask.

She carefully removed the blue jacket from the trunk and checked the hip pockets for coins or anything valuable. They were empty, so she found a coat hanger and hung the jacket on a display along with some counterfeit items a previous manager had purchased from a thief. She typed up a little card and posted it next to the jacket: *Authentic jacket worn by US Army captain (sic) during surrender talks.*

Then she locked the doors and went to lunch.

Chapter Nineteen

The third attempt at closing was a failure, also.

The first two had been total calamities.

At the first one, there was no title and no title insurance, and the closing attorney stood up and held up his hands like he was under arrest and said he wasn't going any further unless there was clear title and history of ownership.

The university attorney put his head on the table and rocked from side to side. He knew he'd get eviscerated by his boss at this debacle, but he wasn't sure where to turn next. *How did it ever get like this, and how do I get us out of it*, he wondered as his spittle dribbled onto the mahogany closing table.

The second closing attempt had been postponed because Reggie needed to move some money around. This was confusing because his funds were available for the first closing that got cancelled. When the funds arrived at the last minute, they came in the form of fourteen billion bitcoins or something from the puzzling land of cryptocurrency. It had taken Reggie nearly sixty days to convert his real US dollars into the crypto stuff, and he had done so after he got a call from his old buddy Tom who had helped him find an agent and who had helped him set up his charitable foundation. He didn't think twice when Tom told him what to do and how to do it and assured him that this is how real estate transactions are done today. With bitcoin, or whatever.

So, Reggie was a tad irritated but not surprised when he was disturbed while on vacation on Jost Van Dyke in the southern Caribbean with three of his favorite girlfriends. His wife didn't know and didn't care, because she was half a world away on the beach at the Del Coronado drinking blender drinks with her latest beau. Reggie, meanwhile, was on his second potent Painkiller rum cocktail at the Soggy Dollar Bar when he got the phone call that his crypto money had been rejected. He immediately called Tom to bitch, but Tom was so upbeat and excited about the player's charity that he lost his edge. That, and he had nearly drained Painkiller number two and was, well, feeling no pain. He told Tom he was busy and asked him to unwind the transfer of his cash to bitcoin or whatever, and Tom said okay, but it might take a couple of months.

And it did.

So, now they were at the closing table for the third time.

Lambeth was there, along with the university attorney and the closing attorney. The electronic transfers from the basketball players, finally and thankfully, popped into the attorney's trust account as promised, and the outgoing transfers to the university's account were ready. The closing documents showed that a two-million-dollar fee had already been paid to a mysterious shell company, but that had happened so long ago and so many other troubling things had happened that nobody even thought about it. The attorney assured Lambeth that the shell company was simply an agent who had facilitated the sale and was being compensated, but he looked over the top of his glasses at Lambeth as if to call total bullshit on that.

The phone on the conference table buzzed, and the closing attorney answered it.

He replaced the receiver and went to the door.

A deputy sheriff greeted him and handed him a manila envelope. He signed the receipt and returned to his seat at the table.

He opened the folder and stared in disbelief. He thumbed through the pages, but everything he needed to see was on the first page.

"What is it?" Lambeth asked.

"An injunction."

Chapter Twenty

The judge and Tom had hashed all this out while embroiled in a desperate battle of golf at Tom's club out in the country where nobody would see them or know they were together.

It was unlikely that anybody would see Tom anyway because he was in the woods most of the time. He was big, tall and strong and could hit the ball forever but rarely knew where it was going to land. He lost his match to the judge today with one bad swing which sent a badly topped tee shot into a ravine. He clamored into the ravine to search for his lost ball, but he heard what he thought was a rattlesnake and abandoned the search. The judge provided him no relief and he lost the hole and eventually a two-dollar bet, but Tom didn't care because he found four old balls in the ravine and that was better than winning a bet.

As they drank vodka and cranberry on the back porch of the club, Tom asked the judge what it would take, theoretically, to get an injunction against the sale of a piece of property. The judge said an injunction could be issued for lots of reasons, but if any citizen made a compelling case that made sense to a judge, the judge could issue a temporary injunction to stop the process while everyone figured out what was going on.

"What if an Indian tribe said they owned property that someone else was selling," Tom said, as he waved for another round of vodka cranberries. "Could they get an injunction?"

The judge looked at Tom with a gleam in his eye and said, "What are you working on?"

Tom had already glommed up the closing of the property a couple of times and had delayed it by nearly a half a year. He was only halfway through his bag of tricks, but this would be a good one.

About three weeks later, Judge Williams convened his courtroom in the shiny new downtown courthouse. He had maneuvered the process to get a particular matter reassigned to his court on this particular day, and no one had argued because nobody knew what it was, but it sounded messy.

The judge knew that the alleged defect in the title was only a rumor at this point, but Tom had told him they were desperately working to find a treaty that awarded the property to the tribe at the end of the Civil War, and they just needed a little time. On the back porch of the club, Tom asked for ninety days; the judge said thirty and they agreed to sixty with one possible extension of thirty more.

In the busy courtroom, verdicts flew back and forth, and attorneys begged, pleaded, argued and lied, and hapless defendants watched their lives change in an instant as the judge pronounced judgement. He had hit his stride dispensing justice for the morning when the Motion for Injunctive Relief hit his desk, and he remembered the vodka cranberry arrangement as well at Tom's support in past elections. He paused for a moment, because he didn't really know what Tom had planned and didn't know what to expect. Perhaps Indians in makeup and headdresses with bows and arrows and feathers and beads and all that stuff you see on TV. With Tom, you never knew.

He was pleasantly surprised when the tribe's attorney arose from the plaintiff's table and introduced herself as Rebecca.

Chapter Twenty-One

The president looked at the first page of the injunction and flung the entire package across the room at his attorney.

The university attorney had been summoned to the president's office and, as always, was unsure whether today's problem was an unwanted pregnancy, a mishap with an offshore bank account, or some legitimate issue with running a major university, which were easier to deal with than the others.

He was flabbergasted by the injunction and that a judge would agree to it.

The president looked like he was going to have a stroke.

"Go fix this!" he shouted at his attorney, in a voice several octaves higher than normal and with a disconcerting tremble. Then he said, almost in a growl, "I need this fixed."

As the university attorney staggered out of the room, digesting what he'd heard, he was troubled that the president was acting crazier than usual, jabbing at his desktop keyboard as if trying to exorcize a demon from the device.

It was a demon, all right.

In addition to all his routine liaisons, the president had finally bedded his ultimate conquest, the early 30s beauty who was the university's deputy fundraiser. Like many women that age, she had figured out who she was and what she liked, and she liked power and money and ambition and enjoyed being around those who had it.

She was the first of his paramours who actually worked for his administration, so his advances to her were slick and technically innocent, until she got his subtle message and invited him to her off-campus apartment, another first for him since his canoodling always occurred in the safe confines of his office.

Their times together were energetic, passionate, and intense, and he would return to his office completely drained and barely able to function the rest of the day, including one day when the Chi O president dropped by and demanded his urgent attention just moments after he flopped into his leather chair. He complied, but barely, leaving the sorority girl frustrated and puzzled that her usual consort was a dud.

But today, he had other problems.

He waved the attorney out of his office and returned to the mess on his desktop.

Two days ago, a messenger strolled into his office, handed him a thumb drive, and left without speaking.

He booted up the thumb drive and gagged at what he saw.

At first, he thought the video was porn. Then, he realized the porn was actually him, and it was his naked ass bouncing around. The camera was carefully positioned to capture his face and that of his lover, and their entangled, naked bodies were there for all to see, warts and flab and everything.

He thought he was going to pass out right there in his office as the video continued until the groaning, moaning denouement of their frolic, when he stood up in full view of the unknown camera and showed his face, his tiny manhood, and everything else.

Man, I need to lose some weight, he thought.

Then the video abruptly ended, and a message appeared on the screen:

Every minute is on video.
Your face, your baby dick, your creepy demands
that she lick your toes.
You'll receive several requests in the coming days.
You must comply or the videos will be everywhere.

BILE ROSE IN HIS THROAT, and he felt like his heart was going to stop.

He sank back in his leather chair, stared at the ceiling, and thought to himself, *Well, it can't get much worse than this.*

The next day, it didn't take the university's

IT geniuses long to unwind the mystery of how and why the entire computer system crashed, leaving a major American educational institution unable to function. No emails, no lesson plans, no anything.

The IT guys immediately found a malware had rapidly infected the system, poisoning every desktop and smart phone as soon as the user opened their first email. It spread throughout the system within minutes.

It took four long hours of investigating, but they finally traced the malware to the president's desktop, where the thumb drive was still sticking out of the machine like a teenager's middle finger flipping off the world. The IT guys unplugged the desktop and confiscated the thumb drive, dramatically placing it in a plastic bag like it was anthrax or what they'd seen on the TV crime shows.

What they couldn't find, and couldn't know was there, was an encrypted fifteen-minute highlight film of the president's clandestine apartment tryst with an elaborate timing mechanism scheduled to deliver the video to every inbox on the university system in two hours, during the lunch hour.

Tom had promised Rebecca that all hell would break loose.

And here it came.

Chapter Twenty-Two

Just before noon, twenty-seven members of the Occoneechee tribe entered the main quad of the campus. They were dressed liked dignified businesspeople, not like TV Indians. They carried two signs. One said, "Our Land is Our Land" and the other said "Stop the Sale." They originally had a third which said, "Scalp the President," but Tom said that was too much, that the Occoneechee had never scalped anyone, and it might be misconstrued to mean the President of the United States that might catch the attention of the Secret Service and distract from their mission.

All of the local television stations and cable news were there, of course. They had been promised some drama on a slow news day, and Tom had cleverly timed the brief march to arrive at the president's office just at noon so all the TV stations would cover it live on their noon broadcasts and titillate their viewers with their beloved "breaking news" tease.

Jim knew to watch the red lights on the camera and, when they blinked on, to begin his speech. He wasn't any good at this, and that made it charming and all the more effective. Rebecca and Tom wrote it for him and rehearsed with him for several days until he could deliver his message that the university was selling land it didn't own, that it was owned by the tribe, they could prove it (well, not yet), and they had earned it by playing a pivotal role in bringing an end to the Civil War, which was not exactly true but sounded good. He also glossed over the point that the tribe had helped the North, which probably wouldn't play well here in the South where legions of rednecks stubbornly clung to the be-liefs of the Confederate cause and considered the federal government to be the war's instigator.

While Jim gave his brief speech, hardly anyone noticed two guys bring a large-screen TV to the edge of the gathering and run a coax cable through the window of one of the ground-level offices of the administrative build-ing. They signed on to a university account and walked away.

When Jim finished his remarks, he had been coached by Tom to move toward the main door, with his followers in tow. Jim knew, because Tom told him, that security would stop him. Jim and his crowd should begin chanting, "Let Us In, Let Us In," for a couple of minutes because it made for good television and would make the university look dumb.

After the chanting, one of Tom's minions organized the TV reporters for individual in-terviews, and all the reporters politely waited on each other because they knew that any PR deal orchestrated by Tom would be interesting and, if they behaved, those tough-to-find dolls at Christmastime wouldn't be so hard to find after all.

The reporters were about to pack up and move on and tear down their lights and cameras and other stuff they use for a live shot.

That's when the large-screen TV flickered to life.

Even the most jaded of the reporters gasped and turned away, then looked back with shock and grins.

The first image was the sweating face, very clearly of the university president.

The rest became local television history.

Chapter Twenty-Three

Rebecca and Tom watched the news coverage on a bank of televisions in his tangled office. He grinned as his eyes flipped from one TV to another, watching the chaos unfold. Rebecca's jaw dropped when the porn video started and the cameramen at the scene were too slow to turn away, thus broadcasting live smut into the homes of their viewers and their children and grandmas. It was perfect.

"I know that video was your doing," she said to Tom. "How'd you get it?"

He looked at her throat area for a minute, like he might be a vampire, and grinned some more.

Then he explained.

"After the slimy bastard raped my daughter, I knew I had to do something to take him out," Tom said, the grin fading from his face. "He was too powerful to fight fair, so this was the answer."

Tom went on to share a tragic tale of his daughter interning in the administrative building during the summer after her sophomore year. She wasn't assigned to the president's office, but he spotted her one day and later asked his secretary to send for her so he could meet her. He arranged for the meeting to be at the end of the day so it would spill over into the time after his staff had left. Then, he did what so many powerful men do to intimidated women; sit on the couch with me, let me hold your hand, tell me your story, blah, blah. It happened before she could resist and was over quickly.

"She was so embarrassed she didn't tell me

for a long time," Tom said sadly. "She finally told me when I was doing some work for the university and preparing some PR crap about what a great guy he is. She couldn't hold it in and told me. Her pain was wrenching, and I was so pissed I was ready to kill him. Seriously. And what's worse is that there was no evidence, no witnesses, and I knew none of his staff would even admit that she'd ever been there. So, he got away with it. Sorta."

Tom then explained how he had helped the university's deputy fundraiser find a safe, comfortable apartment when she moved to town, and then helped her find a reliable, honest housekeeper who would show up on time and not steal her jewelry. The housekeeper he recommended worked for several of his clients, and made extra money keeping Tom informed on what was going on in their lives and homes.

Shortly after Tom's daughter told him about the rape, the housekeeper was in Tom's office updating him on the activity at everyone's house, including what kind of mail was stacked on their kitchen counters, the balances in the checkbooks in their desk drawers, messages on their answering machines and other useful intelligence. Occasionally, they would leave their desktops logged in and she could look at what they'd been doing on their computers, including making car payments for children and illicit girlfriends, watching smut, and other interesting stuff.

She then told Tom that during the middle of her regular shift at the fundraiser's apartment (she had just finished snooping through her desk), the fundraiser rushed in without notice and frantically ordered her to wrap it up and go home and said she would be paid for the entire job. The housekeeper still had her cleaning junk all over the apartment, so she quickly as she could gathered her bucket and mop and sprays and vacuum, but it wasn't quickly enough. Before she could make her exit, the reason for the big rush rushed in himself, startled to find a housekeeper in the way and slowing things down.

"Here's his picture," the housekeeper said to Tom, handing him her smartphone.

The photo was at an odd angle, but the housekeeper was good at this kind of thing and would get a nice cash reward in a few minutes because she had snapped a secret photo of the university president.

Tom put it together instantly and recognized the opportunity he needed.

A friend at a furniture store helped him find a table lamp exactly like the one in the fundraiser's bedroom, a selection made more convenient because of the excellent photo of the lamp snapped by the housekeeper. One of Tom's operatives then took a few days to install a tiny camera, microphone and transmitter into the replacement lamp, which the housekeeper placed on the table in the bedroom. What was so funny was the transmitter was linked to the fundraiser's own wi-fi, which beamed the hi-def signal live and in color into a small control room at Tom's office, where it was dutifully recorded for future use.

It took a couple of adjustments by the housekeeper on subsequent visits to get the camera angle just right. They had plenty of opportunities to get it just right because the university president wasn't the only one stopping by the fundraiser's apartment to put a flabby ass on TV.

"I wasn't sure exactly how I was going to use the nasty videos," Tom told a dumbstruck Rebecca, "until the Indians came to town."

Chapter Twenty-Four

Jim was still steaming when they reached the forest.

He was so angry that he almost couldn't speak after the initial meeting to plan the search for the gold.

But this had been part of Tom's deal with Rebecca. He would help her and Jim sow the seeds of discontent, stir up trouble, muddy the waters, cause great confusion and doubt about the sale of the forest, and he would do it for free, pro bono, largely to stick a proverbial knife in the flabby belly of the feckless university president, in exchange for what was starting today.

Tom wanted a chance to find the gold, and he knew just the guys who could do it, and they were here today.

Tom outlined the terms of the deal. The fortune hunters would get fifty percent of whatever they found, the tribe would get twenty, and Tom would get the rest. He didn't offer anything to Rebecca, and she asked for nothing.

He didn't believe it was necessary to share with the others that his share would be split evenly and discretely with his mentor and friend who was a member of the US Congress, just as a sort of insurance policy to keep the politician focused on what was important in coming weeks.

When he heard the terms, Jim erupted.

"This gold belongs to my people!" he shouted. "What gives you the right to it? This is so typical of how we're treated! Everything we have is taken from us!"

Tom's normal jovial temperament immediately evaporated.

"Wait just a minute," he said, glaring at

Jim. "Right now, you have exactly one hundred percent of nothing. You don't know where to look for it, how to look for it, or even what you're looking for.

"Your people," he continued with a slightly sarcastic tone, "have had several generations to search for it and, as best I can tell, have done nothing but talk about it and all the injustices they've endured."

"Well, today we're taking action. We may not find anything, but without these professionals and without me bringing them here, you'd still be sitting on your papoose counting your hundred percent of nothing at all."

There was silence in the group as Tom let his lecture sink in with Jim, who looked at the ground and said nothing.

Now, they all stood at the edge of the forest, at a gate fashioned out of a round piece of iron stretching across the tiny road, a rutted lane used by Jim for his patrols, for access to the forest for fire protection and for university researchers. The first fifty feet or so was covered with small pieces of burned-out coal debris from the university's old power plant, which was shuttered decades ago after a period of great irony when the professors and students at the great university preached loudly and often against fossil fuels and typed their manifestos in offices warmed and on computers powered by the nastiest fuel on earth.

Rebecca and Tom where there, along with Jim, who had brought Roscoe, and the two fortune hunters.

They looked at Tom. *Where do we even start,* their eyes said.

Over the years, the two fortune hunters standing on the edge of the forest today had found gold, silver, sunken ships filled with treasure, and boxes of cash. Their greatest discovery was a Union schooner that had run aground near the end of the Civil War in a tidal creek near modern day Hilton Head, South Carolina.

As the story went, the small crew of the schooner knew the war was ending, and the confederates they were supposed to fight had disappeared except for occasional harmless pot shots from the shoreline when they sailed up the nameless rivers they were supposed to patrol.

The schooner's crew decided it was time to make a profit while they still had the chance and a government-owned boat. They developed an audacious plan to pillage the elegant waterfront mansions along the South Carolina coast, a plan that was opposed by their captain who was simply eager to take his boat home even though he had no way of communicating with his leadership to know when that time had come.

His crew grew weary of his reluctance, so they gave him the choice to be chained to the stern rail of his own boat, or swim ashore and make his way home. He chose the latter, and the mutineers moved on without him. As a side note, the history of this incident revealed that the captain never made it home and was declared killed in action even though his body was never found. He just disappeared. His family revealed that, even though he was a ship's captain, he didn't know how to swim, so the legend presumed that he drowned on his way to shore from his mutinied vessel.

The mutineers' plan was largely unsuccessful; by the time they arrived to do their ransacking, most of the mansions had already been stripped of their valuables by Union infantry and cavalry who were roaming the area. On their climactic day as mutineers and criminals, they encountered a Union infantry officer who told them that the war was over and that everyone needed to go home. When he learned the schooner had no captain, he ordered the mutineers to turn the vessel over to his command so that his unit could sail back to Charleston in style and avoid a miserable march through the mosquito-infested swamps of the South Carolina low country filled with back-water toothless lowlifes who would never surrender the South. He knew that some of his men would be killed by snipers on the march.

The mutineers refused to relinquish their boat, and a brief scuffle broke out when the Union officer realized that these sailors were likely mutineers. Several of the lead mutineers were quickly killed because they had no weapons to speak of, and the others were put in chains. The Union officer now controlled the schooner, and his troops quickly loaded their gear and their prizes, four trunks loaded with confederate gold, much to the relief of the mules who were turned loose once they were relieved of their burden. The Union troops had captured the gold after a gun battle with the crew of a small confederate train that was trying to make its way to Atlanta. Their plan was to turn over three trunks to the federal government and disburse the fourth amongst themselves.

The voyage was a short one.

They had killed the three sailors who actually knew how to maneuver the schooner, who understood about wind and currents and tides and navigation and the complexity of sails. As soon as they cast off, the schooner was moving on its own, bumping into the shoreline and turning lazy circles as the river current determined where the boat was going. The soldiers managed to set a sail, but that made matters worse as the breeze and current carried the vessel into open water. As the vessel swirled and meandered, a small thunderstorm developed over the steamy land, and moved toward them. The sudden wind filled the sail, and pushed the boat in a new direction, toward an island in the middle of the river.

The storm was quick but violent, with blinding rain, a moment of hail. The Union officer discovered the schooner would respond if one of his soldiers leaned on the rudder, but it wasn't enough to actually control it. At the height of the brief storm, the heavy wind pushed the uncontrolled vessel into sandy shoals at the island's point, which ripped a hole in the starboard bow and caused the schooner to lurch onto its right side. The wind continued, coming off the port side and filling the only sail, causing the schooner to roll over on its damaged side and quickly begin to sink.

There was no time to free the chained mutineers, so they drowned, squirming in their restraints, screaming for their lives. In the sudden chaos, there was no time to save the treasure, so it was lost.

The Union officer and his soldiers swam for shore, but they were murdered in a barrage of gun fire by the island's residents, freed slaves who had learned to trust no one who was white and wore a uniform.

The fortune hunters found the treasure after a three-year search that was helped by a rudimentary map that had been drawn by one of the island dwellers to mark their various conquests over those who tried to infiltrate their island and a two-year battle with the government of South Carolina, which contended it owned the gold since it had been stolen from a train in that state and was discovered in that state. But the federal law was on the side of the fortune hunters.

As a result, they were rich beyond measure, had the capital to invest in a new adventure, and had the savvy, technology and intuition.

Except this time, they had no map.

Chapter Twenty-Five

It was a coincidence that Rebecca arrived at the Bennett Place at the same time as the fire department.

Her search of the boxes saw many references to this place, and brought her to this tiny memorial park, which was now surrounded by small ranch-style homes on what was once expansive farmland, sold by the farmers in the nineteen fifties when they needed cash and the city was crawling in that direction.

The small site included a log cabin, which was now engulfed in flames, and a two-story-tall granite monument that had the word

"Unity" carved into it to mark the history that occurred at Bennitt's kitchen table, even though the place is now spelled Bennett Place after a misspelling somewhere in history and even though there's not anything authentic about the house. Indeed, the rumor was that Bennitt's farm was originally located a ways down the road but rich people in the early nineteen hundreds said this was the spot so history wouldn't interfere with their farming.

If she had come yesterday, Rebecca could have accomplished her goal of snooping around to see if the artifacts housed in the tiny log cabin held any clues to the missing treaty.

Now, those artifacts were being hustled out of the burning building by firefighters and dumped in a pile in the yard as their colleagues began to spray water into the building through the open front door and through a window on the back. No one had yet cordoned off the scene, so Rebecca moved closer to the building and to where the fire captain and two of his men were motioning at the top of the stone chimney, which had been damaged and several stones knocked loose and fallen to the ground.

"Last night's thunderstorm," the captain said, "must've smoldered all night."

As Rebecca eavesdropped, a woman who looked like a weary librarian approached the captain.

"I'm the docent here," she told the captain, a stunned look on her face. "We don't have a manager because of budget cuts. I'm the only staff person, so I guess I'm in charge."

The captain told her it looked like lightning hit the chimney and caused the fire, but he asked her if there was anything flammable or electrical in the cabin that could've started a fire, and she said the only electrical items were her laptop, which she had with her, and a coffee pot that had been stolen while she was furloughed. The captain said they would investigate further, then moved off to make sure the conflagration didn't spread to the adjoining neighborhood.

The docent stood still, clearly unable to process what she was seeing and unable to decide what she should do next. She spoke into her phone for a moment, letting some bureaucrat in state government know about the fire, then stood and watched the firefighters douse the small remaining flames.

Rebecca walked over to her, looked her in the eyes, and said she was sorry for what had happened.

The docent looked back and said she didn't know what to do next.

"Is there anything I can help you do?" Rebecca asked softly.

The docent gestured toward the pile of antique furniture and other artifacts that had been rescued, some had scars from the fire, others were smoldering, and some of the clothing items were wadded up in a pile.

"I need to do something with these things," she said to Rebecca, as if hoping Rebecca would tell her what to do. "I don't know where to put them so they're safe."

Rebecca had no idea what to do, and the pile of stuff looked like the dregs of a bad yard sale and the only safe place would be a dumpster. She immediately regretted inserting herself into this problem.

She looked around, and spotted a maintenance shed in the corner of the historical site.

"What about there?" Rebecca asked the docent.

"Uh, okay," the docent replied.

In her charming way, Rebecca approached a couple of the firefighters who were resting and, in an artificial way, coyly and with a sweet smile asked them if they would help move the furniture. They agreed, of course, after checking out every inch of her from brunette hair to her loafers, pausing momentarily on her boobs and ass. After moving on, they poked at the debris to make sure it wasn't harboring some random sparks that would burn down the rest of the historical site.

That left the pile of small artifacts and some clothing, all of which smelled like smoke and some of which was damp from the fire department's hoses.

"A lot of this is fake," the docent said, looking out of the corner of her eyes at Rebecca, as if she was revealing a deep secret. "Years ago, they bought a bunch of it from a dealer just to have something to display. And some of it is stolen. We bought it from a thief. I'm not sure which is which."

She sifted through the pile of clothing and pulled out a uniform jacket.

"But this is not," she said, handing it to Rebecca, who reluctantly took it. It was wool, with US Army buttons, and it stank from age and smoke. The docent quickly told her the story about how the coat came to Bennett Place, and the letter from the innkeeper in New York.

Rebecca didn't want to be rude and just toss the stinking jacket back on the pile, so she held it up and halfway pretended to examine it. Instead of wadding it up for a return to the pile, she began to carefully fold it so it could be stored properly.

That's when she heard something crinkle.

She pressed her hand against the jacket and another crinkle. It wasn't the sound of folding wool, but the sound of paper being crunched.

Rebecca held up the jacket by one of its shoulders with one hand and pressed some more with the other to find what was making the sound. She cringed slightly as she slid her hand inside the coat and moved around until she located an inside pocket.

She could tell it was a piece of paper, and she looked to see if the docent was watching her, and she was.

"What is it?" the docent asked.

"Nothing," Rebecca replied, sliding her hand from inside the jacket. She carefully folded the jacket and added it to a small pile of debris that she walked to the shed.

Inside the shed, and momentarily alone and out of sight, she slipped the paper out of the jacket. She had no jacket of her own, and her purse and briefcase were in the car, so she crammed the paper into her blouse and sort of shifted it around to her right side where it might not be so obvious.

She returned to the docent's desperate situation and helped a little more. Then, as quickly as she could, she fled the scene.

Chapter Twenty-Six

Leon knew it was the end of him and Rebecca.

Of course, there had never been a beginning to him and Rebecca, nor a middle.

There was never a place in the life of a woman like Rebecca for a guy like Leon, but he had cherished every moment of their time together. It had been a fruitless adventure for the two of them through his tiny part of the nation's archives. As long as she was showing up every day, there was hope for them both to find what they sought.

He had delayed her departure for several

days, deliberately obscuring some of his treasures and sending them down rabbit holes. He loved being with her, in the bowels of his warehouse.

And now she was gone. She told Leon how much she appreciated his time, then shook his hand like a business partner. A kiss on the cheek would've been nice, he thought, but he was too awkward to ask for one.

Then she was off to continue her search, off to Appomattox, and probably out of his life.

He returned to the work that he had delayed while helping Rebecca. He had been tasked to assist a history professor at the University of Virginia, who was writing a book about the art of the Civil War, not the fine art of the painters who had created all those magnificent and colorful recreations of battle scenes with steely-eyed, heroic generals aboard magnificent horses and the despair of their soldiers dying in the field.

Instead, the professor was assembling a book of the sketches and doodlings of soldiers, common folk, and others who recorded their

Civil War experiences with a piece of charcoal or a rudimentary pencil of the time or a quill and ink and sent them to their families or preserved them in journals. Actually, as usual, the professor was doing very little of the work. He had a small team of graduate students in the warehouse getting their hands dirty every day, prying open box after box of memorabilia and searching for the right kind of art for the book. His thesis was that the colorful paintings of the era glorified the war and masked the pain and suffering and were commissioned and painted after the war. The sketches of the actual participants, however, were done in real time as events occurred and would give a more realistic picture of how the actual participants viewed the war and how it impacted their lives.

If they could find a few hundred of them, it would make a nice book that would ease some of the pressure on him as an academic to publish, publish, publish without having do any significant research or writing.

The grad students had just about exhausted all of Leon's resources, and didn't have enough material for a short magazine article much less the glorious, and profitable, coffee table book envisioned by their professor.

Leon had been cranking through his computer cross-referencing for journals, notebooks with art in them and loose sketches, and had run out of leads for the students. Then, he thought back to his depressing days in Maplewood and remembered a collection of framed art that had been stored in the dank basement for decades and which county leaders had ordered him to sell at auction when they calculated the frames were worth something and the art wasn't.

He wasn't sure why that memory popped into his mind, but it prompted him to ask his mainframe for any collection of framed Civil War drawings. He'd never thought to search for framed items, and it apparently never occurred to the grad students either.

His search revealed twelve boxes. The grad students were relieved.

As expected, the frames were rotten and in disrepair in nearly every box, and there were only a few drawings the grad students thought would pass muster with the professor. Leon gave them permission to remove the drawings from their moldy frames, photograph them with their smartphones for the professor to see, and then place them in special envelopes which Leon documented. They would be allowed to remove them from the archives under the terms of the professor's research agreement, have them professionally reproduced for the book's publication, then return them to Leon's safe keeping for the rest of all time.

While the students picked their way through history, Leon returned to his cubicle to catalog some items and catch up on other work that had gone undone while he was distracted by Rebecca.

The students sent for him; they found something they needed help with.

It was a sketch, likely done with charcoal or pencil, and at the bottom it said, "Bennit house, April 1865." The writing was smudged, and the drawing was amateurish, like most of what the students were looking for and finding. Leon looked at the drawing and assumed it was someone's rendition of the surrender that took place at Bennett Place, and the scene depicted was probably Johnston surrendering to Sherman. The artist had drawn Sherman with a defiant look on his face, and a sad look on the face of his counterpart.

"Turn it over," one of the grad students said.

Leon slowly turned over drawing, careful to not further smudge it.

There was writing on the reverse, a letter perhaps. The artist had used the only paper he could find to make his drawing of the historic surrender, and now Leon furrowed his brow as he examined the words.

"Holy shit," he cried, startling the grad students and anyone else who was in the silent warehouse. "You won't believe what we've found."

He dashed away from the stunned students and ran to his desk. He dialed Rebecca, misdialing the first time in his excitement, and getting her voice mail when he finally dialed the right numbers.

"You won't believe this," he said.

Chapter Twenty-Seven

Jim had expected the request for a while and wasn't surprised when it came. The associate assistant dean of the forestry school would be conducting a tour and needed a key to one of the gates closest to campus. He didn't tell Jim who was taking the tour, but Jim knew.

Jim dropped off a key at the appointed hour, but it was the wrong key, of course. Jim had changed the locks on all the gates at Tom's suggestion, and there was only one good key and it was in his pocket. Tom had made several suggestions. The key was only one of them.

A few days later, the tour group that included Reggie, his investment partners, and the associate assistant dean arrived at the gate in Reggie's Land Rover with its cool blacked-out wheels and vanity plate REG1. Reggie grimaced as he saw the muddy entrance to the forest. His Land Rover wouldn't be spotless for long.

The associate assistant dean got out of the back seat to unlock the gate. The plan was to cruise around the forest's fire trails in the Land Rover and get a feel for the property. Nobody could remember who suggested this, but the idea was to keep the investors excited about the deal while everything was going wrong and kill some time and make the guys feel like something was actually happening while the experts tried to figure out how to salvage the mess.

The Land Rover's exquisite sound system was thumping, and the passengers were grooving to the tunes as they waited for the associate assistant dean to unlock the gate and let them in.

They watched his hunched-over figure with his back to them take way too long.

Reggie turned down the tunes and lowered his window.

"What's wrong, man?" he yelled from the driver's seat.

The hunched-over figure half turned around.

"Key won't work, or the lock's busted, or something," came the reply.

Reggie slumped in his seat and stroked the two-day growth on his chin. *Typical of this whole deal,* he thought, *something is always, always messed up.*

Reggie got out of the car, took the key from the associate assistant dean, and tried wiggling it around in the lock, but it was no use. He came close to breaking the key off he wrenched it so violently.

"What'd we do now," he asked, glaring at the lock.

"We could walk," said the dean, looking out of the corner of his eye at Reggie and halfway cowering as if Reggie was going to cold cock him.

Reggie returned to the Land Rover, and after a brief yelling match, his fellow investors unfolded themselves from their leather heated and cooled seats.

"Man," one of them complained to Reggie, "these sneaks are custom made, not even in the stores yet. I'm gonna ruin them in these shitty woods."

Reggie looked at him with total disgust.

"You didn't even pay for them," he said angrily. "Friggin' Nike gave them to you. How many do you have in your closet?"

Reggie didn't wait for an answer but headed toward the iron rod that served as a gate and blocked the road, and gracefully stepped over it. His fellow investors followed along with the little dean.

They walked up a short hill. At the top of the hill, the road curved slight to the left.

And that's when they stopped.

They didn't know who or what it was, but it was Jezz.

She was in the middle of the little road, in all her glory.

She was magnificent.

She appeared eight feet tall, not including the feathers and wild hair teased up as far as it would go. Her height was secretly enhanced by a little stool that was hidden by her stunning leather dress that went all the way to the ground. She was draped in turquoise necklaces and everything else she could think of. Four small fires encircled her, each of them smoldering, their light blue smoke swirling around her and adding a mystical element to her, a lucky twist because any slight breeze would've blown away the smoke and ruined the moment.

When she saw the visiting ensemble come to a halt, she threw her head back, dramatically flung her arms into the air, and half-shouted and half-sung some unintelligible noise that may have sounded like a war chant. The leather tassels hanging from her sleeves reached all the way to the ground, adding more elegance to the movement of Jezz's sweeping arms.

In a wonderful coincidence, a huge red-tail hawk who lived nearby chose this moment to become enamored with the craziness on the top of Jezz's head and began sailing back and forth above her, now and then taking a soft dive toward her. To the tourists who stood spellbound in the dirt road, it actually looked like Jezz was controlling the bird's movement.

Reggie and the boys didn't know what to do. They looked at the associate assistant dean, but he was frantically glancing around as if he expected his body to be pierced by arrows at any moment.

"Is this the Indians we heard about?" asked the one with the sneaks that already were soiled.

"I don't know what's going on," Reggie said, eyes wide and wild.

"Come closer," Jezz shouted and waved her arms theatrically toward the confused group as the hawk swept by.

"I ain't going near her," said Mr. Sneakers. He was third-generation Haitian, and he had heard plenty in his life about Caribbean witchcraft and voodoo and all that. "I'm outta here."

"I ain't afraid," Reggie said and took a step in her direction.

"Welcome to my forest, and to my world," Jezz shouted in a sing-song way, moving her graceful body and waving her arms above her head. The hawk settled onto the limb of a long-leaf pine, about forty feet away.

Jezz held tightly in her right hand a couple of ounces of gunpower that had been cut with black pepper. The gunpower came from a some of old forty-four caliber shells that Jim gave her and helped her remove the bullets to get at the powder.

As Reggie took his first tentative step, Jezz again dramatically waved her arm, shouted an incoherent chant, and gracefully dumped the mixture in her hand on the little fire in front of her.

The small explosion nearly knocked her off her stool, which would have ruined the effect, and the white smoke completely obscured her vision of what was happening down the road.

When it cleared, the tour group had re-treated in great haste toward the safety of the Land Rover, and the hawk had disappeared.

Chapter Twenty-Eight

They all sat in the Senator's office, with its splendid view of the Capitol rotunda, as a phalanx of twenty-something staffers dashed in and out in breathless self-importance, telling their member what he needed to know to get through another day of bravely and selfishly serving his constituents.

Rebecca, Tom and Jim sat on his sofa, and he finally told the twenty-somethings to shut the door and leave them alone.

Tom was on familiar ground because years ago he had been on the staff of the Senator sitting across from him. At the feet of this man he had learned many of his tricks, and then he had graduated to a level of trickery and expertise that made the old lawmaker smile.

"Is this really real?" the Senator asked.

"Absolutely," Tom said. "Jim and his people own that forest. No doubt about it."

The Senator leaned back and stared at them. The document Leon had found was sealed in a special clear envelope to prevent damage, but they could still see it clearly. They reviewed it line by line, then they showed him the research they had quickly done. It didn't completely verify the role the Occoneechee had played in the war, because it had been so secretive and undocumented and controlled only by one general, but there was enough anecdotal history and enough varied sources that you could say it was true, most likely.

They also showed him the expert analysis of the signature. It matched Sherman's signature on the surrender document precisely.

"But it was never ratified," Rebecca added.

"And you want me to do that," the Senator said.

All three answered yes in unison.

"This will be a tough one," the lawmaker said as he did the legislative gymnastics in his head. The university will pitch a fit, and he grinned as he thought about the university president spitting up blood.

Tom had kept the Senator updated on the plans to develop the forest and had informed every time there had been a setback in those plans. He never went into detail about the setbacks, and never revealed he was the source of so many of them. He didn't have to.

The lawmaker continued his stream of conscious analysis of the situation. "There's a real prejudice against Indian tribes in Congress," he admitted. "They don't have much clout, and there's a real reluctance to recognize them, to expand their reservations, or to allow them to grow economically by building casinos and other things on the reservations."

"It's like nothing has changed since the Trail of Tears," the lawmaker said. "It's sad and racist, but it's the political reality I've got to deal with as I try to convince the bunch of fools in Senate to ratify this thing."

He then looked at Jim.

"What are you gonna do with that forest if it clearly belongs to your people?" he asked. "How will you benefit?"

Jim honestly didn't know. There was really no one in his tiny tribe he could trust to help him think this through, so he hadn't shared it. They were a destitute, uneducated group who simply didn't have the experience or knowledge to contribute much to the discussion.

"A casino? Sell it? Develop it?" the Senator asked.

Jim thought for a moment, aware of the enormity of this moment in his life and in the history of his tribe.

He thought he might throw up right there on the Senator's oriental rug, but he choked back the bile and thought for a moment.

He had killed real people who had spoiled and soiled his forest, pulled the trigger himself and watched them die, not so much because they had threatened and terrorized him, but because of what they had done to the peace and beauty of a forest he loved and which he believed deep in his heart belonged to him and his people and shouldn't be chopped down and bulldozed so some rich assholes can play a stupid game.

He cleared his throat and locked eyes with the Senator.

"We want it just like it is," he said. "It's value to us is the forest, the trees and the streams and the animals. We want to walk where our people walked and keep the land just like it was. We want nothing beyond that."

The Senator stared at him, the wheels turning in his complicated brain.

"So, if this treaty is approved and your people own the land, you're not going to monetize it or capitalize on it?" the Senator asked.

"That is correct," Jim said, not exactly sure what those words meant.

"Then we can do this," the Senator said and called in his top aide.

Chapter Twenty-Nine

Nothing is ever simple or straightforward in Washington.

Over the next three days, Jim and Rebecca got a civics lesson they would never forget and, in Jim's case, barely understand.

The Senator welcomed them to join him in a series of meetings and negotiations, including with the Senate bill drafting manager who, despite his seniority and experience, had never converted a handwritten Civil War treaty into the legislative format required for ratification. In fact, no one alive on Capitol Hill had ever done it.

It was virgin territory for everyone, which meant there were no rules, which meant the Senator could be creative. They copied pertinent parts of historic treaty ratification between the US and other nations, but this one was actually simple because the general had been specific and clear about what the US was giving to the Indians, even though the precise description of the property involved was totally vague.

By now, Rebecca had registered as an official lobbyist for the Nation of the Occoneechees, and the Senator and his aide left it to her to work out the specific language.

Next came a series of other strategic meetings.

The Senator had never been seen as a total friend of the environment, even though he at heart was an environmentalist but had never been a lead sponsor of a significant pro-environment legislation. So, it was with some suspicion that the lead lobbyist for the Sierra Club was summoned to the Senator's conference room, where she was introduced to Jim and Rebecca.

"What would you think if we could take two thousand acres of prime Carolina forest off the table forever," asked the Senator, in his blunt way of starting a conversation.

The Sierra Club lobbyist, a short weeble-wobble woman with unkempt hair, the poster child for an environmentalist, was mean as a snake, trusted no one, and usually could hardly conceal her contempt for members of Congress who she viewed as corrupt and who would rather dump raw sewage in the Fountain of Youth than save a garter snake.

"Well," she said, with a career of skepticism guiding her response, "I'm listening."

The Senator broadly outlined the issue for a few minutes, then turned the floor over for the next hour to Jim and Rebecca to talk about what it meant to Jim's people. The Senator had learned decades ago that it was always better for local people to explain issues and what they meant to them. For this meeting, he told Jim and Rebecca to focus on how this arrangement would be an environmental windfall and to give the Sierra Club a list of as many endangered plants and species as possible that might be found in the forest.

This was one of the most amazing opportunities the Sierra Club had ever heard of in a growing metro area.

"What do you need from us?" she asked the Senator, her voice nearly quivering with uncharacteristic excitement.

He was clear in his response about what he needed, including a vow of secrecy, which was readily agreed to.

Other meetings with similar agendas were hurriedly arranged, including a critical one with the Conservation Council, whose leadership was as stunned as the Sierra Club to hear the plan and eagerly agreed to whatever the Senator wanted. He was clear with them also, and they promised their support and silence.

The best legislation is that which is drafted in the dark, explained in unintelligible code, allies established in secret and the done deal sprung on unexpected, hapless victims before they even know there's an issue to be discussed. It's difficult for political opponents to organize, develop and deliver their message and have any influence on the outcome of a debate if they have no idea the debate is getting ready to occur.

The Senator did his thing, strategically moving among his colleagues, explaining what was going to happen and how he needed their vote, often reminding them of favors owed and alliances needed on fights yet to come. The only pushback came from lawmakers representing states that already had recognized Indian tribes and pulsating, popular casinos, but their resistance largely faded when they were assured that the ratification of this treaty essentially prevented any sort of development, which would include casinos.

As he swirled, he was accompanied by the tribe's new lobbyist. He occasionally asked her for privacy when he had to deal with a particular ornery colleague, and she would step aside and patiently wait. She realized that she was actually adding very little value to this process, but the Senator felt it was helpful to have someone from home who might answer a question that he didn't the know the answer to.

And, Rebecca was willing to be patient.

One of the obscure provisions in the ratification document created a perpetual conservation easement for a piece of property adjacent to the tribe's forest, identified in the legislation only by its tax identification number. Essentially, this provision would put a literal fence around her family farm, prohibit it from ever being developed or sold, and eventually deed it to the Conservation Council when it was no longer needed for its current use. Rebecca understood that she was sacrificing a good chunk of her inheritance, but it was worth it to ensure that her father and Charlie could live out their days without greedy developers banging on the door with threats and tricks.

While the Senator moved around, so did his staffers, brilliant and eager and young, as they practiced their skills on their counterparts around the Capitol, explaining the details and the deals and how the ratification worked, so when their dingbat bosses needed to be briefed ahead of the vote the youngsters could steer them in the right direction.

At the same time, the Sierra Club and Conservation Council lobbyists made their rounds,

giving key lawmakers who were their sup-
porters a heads up about the ratification and to
ensure them that any concerns about recog-
nizing another tribe were mitigated by the significant environmental prize in the legislation.
These groups had potent grassroots operations
that could be mobilized in an instant to call
lawmaker's offices, but the Senator asked them
to withhold this strike capability; he didn't
think it was necessary because he was sensing
plenty of support and no organized opposition
to speak of, and he thought it actually might be
counterproductive by tipping off some foes
about what was going to happen and give them
time to organize some trouble.

Congress moves agonizingly slow, or not at
all most of the time, because its members are
paralyzed by fear of losing their seats in the
next election if they take a stand on anything.
There will always be somebody back home
who oppose that anything. But, under the right
circumstances, and with a powerful legislator at
the helm who's done many favors for the leadership who decides what lives and dies on
Capitol Hill, and with an issue that has been

thoroughly lobbied and explained, the velocity of the place can be stunning.

And so, this was the case with the treaty ratification. A series of baffling and head-spinning motions were made on the floor and seconded, allowing it to skip many of the steps taught in civics class. Rules were set aside on voice votes by lawmakers who weren't even listening, and suddenly the ratification of a Civil War treaty was on the floor, ready for a discussion and a vote.

The Senator had cleverly worked with the leadership so that the ratification would hit the floor just before lunch on a Thursday. His distracted colleagues would be more focused on making it to lunch at The Monocle or looking at their watches to make sure they didn't miss their flight home for the weekend because, after all, three days of legislating is enough for one week.

He began his brief speech with a history lesson of the Occoneechee's valuable assistance in the Civil War – he glossed over the part about them helping the Union side for fear of alienating his Southern colleagues who still simmered about the war's outcome, especially the South Carolina delegation which would start the war again if they could. He described the property and how the ratification document required a proper survey because none existed but that under no circumstances would the size of the property be less than the acreage to which all parties agreed. He then explained how this was a commitment made by the federal government and, but for a lost document, would've been honored two generations ago, and it was now time to make things right.

He concluded with a flourish, made a motion to call the question, and thus ended the debate, which was eagerly agreed to by his distracted and impatient colleagues.

As he began his oratory, the Capitol Hill lobbyist for the university was in his office, working on some meaningless position paper. C-Span was on his TV, but the sound was muted. He'd been hired a few years ago by the university president who wanted for the first time to have a presence on the Hill. The lobbyist was a Hill lifer; he rarely went to the university, wasn't a part of the community, and most of the time was completely out of touch with nearly everything. He also rarely left his office, preferring to do his lobbying by phone and by position paper, which meant he was about as effective as an empty roll of toilet paper.

His mobile phone buzzed, irritating him.

"Are you listening to the floor?" his junior lobbyist asked.

"No, why?" the lobbyist responded, not looking up from his keyboard.

"They're debating something about our research forest," the junior lobbyist replied.

"What forest?" asked the lobbyist.

The junior lobbyist was trained at the state level, where lobbyists never turn their back on anything, never leave the building if lawmakers are in session, and assume something bad is going to happen if they take more than twenty minutes for lunch. It was a real contrast to the style of her boss, which explained why she was well-known and respected and he wasn't. She didn't know much about the forest, but she recognized some of the landmarks being discussed because she was tuned into the university and its work and its community.

"I gotta go find out," she said, swiping off the call.

She moved at battle speed through the crowded hallway and anterooms outside the chamber, but, by the time she found a copy of the ratification and figured out what was going on, the debate had ended, the vote was taken, and the body adjourned for the weekend as the big doors were thrust open and lawmakers spewed out, heading in a multitude of directions, trying to avoid obstacles like junior lobbyists who were trying to figure out what just happened.

With a copy of the ratification in hand, the junior lobbyist sat on a bench to quickly digest what the legislation said and what it meant to her client.

The blood drained from her face as she skimmed the document.

The United States Senate had just agreed that it was the policy of the nation to give the university forest to an Indian tribe.

Forever, as in perpetual.

It could never be developed. And, if she was reading it correctly, any current research or activity currently underway could continue, which was good news, she thought. Then came the bad news that within one hundred twenty days of passage, anyone conducting any research or activity was required by federal law, my goodness, to enter into a contract with the tribe for the continuation of such activity and that such a contract would require proper remuneration to the tribe consistent with the value received.

How did this happen, she wondered.

She felt like she'd been stabbed in the heart. How could they miss something like this? It became law without them even knowing it! She wanted to cry but had been told by a long-ago boss to never cry where they can see you, so crying would have to wait.

She called back her boss, who listened in stunned silence.

He hung up and dialed the university president.

Chapter Thirty

The search for the gold was pretty sophisticated, which it had to be since there was no map.

The hunters first arranged for a helicopter flyover of the entire property and used a complex camera system to photograph every inch of the forest from the air. The photos were assembled on the wall of their rented office, and when they were pieced together, it gave them a gigantic photo montage of the forest. They spent several days poring over the photos with magnifying glasses, looking for anything that might give them a clue as to the gold's whereabouts. The only interesting thing was a couple of coeds skinny dipping in one of the streams and waving to the helicopter. The fortune hunters made a special note about this location for later on.

They then overlaid the photos with a grid, and every block in the grid was ten yards square and assigned a number. Their intent was to examine every grid, every inch, and literally leave no stone unturned.

The hired a drone operator and ordered him to fly his drone at tree-top level over areas where their instincts suggested, but they spotted nothing that would suggest hidden treasure.

They prioritized the grids and brought in their ground-penetrating radar, most often used by law enforcement to find cadavers and criminal stuff, and it would certainly find a chest of gold as long as it wasn't buried under a granite rock.

They hired a dozen students from the university, gave them quick training on how to search a grid block, and set them loose with the tedious task of walking over every step of every grid in every inch of the forest.

If it was there, they would find it.

For a guy who liked action and immediate gratification, the process was torturous for Tom. He pleaded with the fortune hunters to move faster, but they said this is how you do it and we'll miss something if we move faster.

Then, to Tom's dismay, they announced they would be gone for a week or longer, and all fortune hunting would be suspended. They were due in court to defend themselves after the state of Utah sued them to take one of their prizes from them, a familiar experience in their business.

It had been one of their biggest scores. During the nation's rapid westward expansion, a train car hauling silver for the US government broke a wheel on a trestle, and tumbled into the river below, pulling with it the back half of the entire train, including the caboose and the luckless conductor inside. The ravine beneath the trestle was narrow and treacherous, and the water was so deep and dark and rapid that every recovery operation had failed, with the failures usually including at least one worker being swept down river to their death.

So, the silver lay in the river bottom for generations, unreachable and untouched until Tom's fortune hunters spent ten million dollars to build a coffer dam in the river, a dramatic feat of engineering that was inspired when one of them read a book about the construction of the Brooklyn Bridge, where coffer dams were used to build the foundations of the bridge's towers.

Their effort was ultimately successful, as they drained the river from around the sunken rail car, with the only casualties including a foreman who lost a leg when a crane collapsed and one of their workers who maintained the tradition of being swept downriver and eventually drowned.

They recovered one hundred and thirteen million dollars in silver, and now an insurance company wanted it all, arguing that the company it once was covered the claim, or part of it, for the missing silver, and thus owned it. This, of course, was a long-shot money grab. The original insurance company had been through a dozen buyouts and mergers and corporate overthrows in the last hundred years, but they'd found some old claim certificates and had a convincing argument. So, the fortune hunters had to defend themselves and admitted to Tom they would see how the trial started and if it didn't look good, they'd cut a deal with the insurers and settle for half, still a payday of astounding proportions.

Tom updated Rebecca and Jim with the frustrating news, and Rebecca told herself now was the time to act.

Chapter Thirty-One

Everyone in the conference room was pissed. They just didn't know who to be pissed at.

"I'm sick of this shit," Reggie said angrily. "I'm sick of lawyers and problems and crazy people in the woods."

Reggie was especially furious because this dream of his seemed to be in serious jeopardy, and he didn't understand enough about it to really know why so many horrible things had happened to his beloved vision for The Eno Club.

He thought about all the great golf that

was likely to never happen, all the beautiful women that wouldn't entertain him and his guests, all the corporate jets that would never land, all the memorable times that seemed to be careening toward disaster.

Then he thought about his money.

"Where's our money?" Reggie loudly demanded of their host, the attorney who would handle the closing if there ever was one. "I mean, where is it right this minute?"

The closing attorney explained how his trust account worked and assured them their money was safe and would be returned if the project never closed. "There had been considerable expenses," he said patronizingly, "and those would be deducted when their initial investment was returned."

"What about the two mill we paid that broker guy?" Reggie asked, getting more frustrated by the minute.

"Umm, I'm not sure about those funds," the closer said, looking around the room for help, finally stopping his gaze on the university attorney who would know about it if anybody did, but he was focused on a spot of ink on his notepad and didn't look up. "We'll have to get back to you on that. I don't have the contract here, but I'm pretty sure that we can demand a refund if the project doesn't fly."

Reggie looked around the room in total disgust at the blank, highly paid faces, including Lambeth, who had changed the scope of the project so much that Reggie didn't even recognize it any more. He looked at another blank face, a title attorney or something like that who had come in with bad news that he simply couldn't get a clear title and now that the Indians had gone public with their claims of ownership, nobody in his business would touch the title insurance requirements of a big piece of property like this.

He then looked at the university attorney, who was just back after being summoned to a meeting at the offices of the Federal Aviation Administration whose officials had heard about a planned landing field on property now owned by the university and made it clear, totally clear, that no such landing field would be approved for use by the university or anyone who may come to own that property because of its proximity to the approach and departures to the local airport, which proudly claimed to be an international airport.

Notably missing from the meeting was the university president, who had shown an unusual personal interest in this project and had been one of its most visible advocates. His attorney explained that he was unavailable today after being summoned to an emergency meeting of the school's board of trustees. The attorney told them he didn't know the subject of the meeting, but he knew in his gut that such meetings never have a happy outcome.

"So, let me see if I can summarize," Lambeth said. "The new plans for the project make sense financially but our investors are unhappy because it doesn't look like their vision. We can't get clear title. A bunch of Indians have us tied in knots because they say the land is theirs. We can't build the landing field. We haven't been able to get a deal on the farm next door. Hell, there might be a nuclear waste dump in the middle of the place we don't know about that somebody's gonna call us about."

As if on cue, the mobile phone of the university attorney buzzed, and he stepped from the room.

When he returned, his face had the ashen hue of a person who had just been hit by car.

"Turn on the local news," he told the host, who opened a cabinet and punched some buttons on a remote control.

It was breaking news at noon on the biggest station in the state which had their excitable government reporter live and on the scene at one of the entrances to the university forest.

The occupants in the conference listened in confusion and anger and disbelief as the reporter described the momentous action taken by the United States Senate just minutes earlier to ratify a Civil War treaty that gave over two thousand acres of property – he swung his arm dramatically to reveal the trees in question – to an Indian tribe. He called them the Oconee Indians, but that was pretty good for local TV journalism.

The reporter then interviewed the tribe's spokesperson, who ironically was a white woman who worked for a PR firm but who articulately told the camera that this was one of the most significant days in the state's history and corrected an overdue problem. The reporter read a statement from the Senator about the honor to help restore the property and dignity of an indigenous people. The reporter signed off with a breathless promise of more breaking news on this landmark legislation to come on their broadcasts at 4, 4:30, 5, 5:30 and 6, and again at 11 and a special half-hour report the next night at 7 that would preempt an Andy Griffith rerun.

When the reporter finished, Reggie angrily flung the only thing he could put his hands on, a coaster that went sailing toward the head of the table. His teammates and fellow investors, sitting at the end of the table, covered their mouths so he couldn't see them laughing, and they shared a knowing look with each other that it was a typical Reggie pass...off the mark.

Chapter Thirty-Two

Rebecca despised meeting in Jim's trailer, but there was no other choice and they needed privacy.

"I have something to show you," she told him after she cleared a spot on his nasty couch and pushed Roscoe aside. "And it's got to be our secret."

Jim was wide-eyed and agreed.

She removed from her briefcase the piece of parchment she'd stolen from the Bennett Place. It was enveloped in a plastic sheath to protect it, and she laid it on Jim's coffee table.

"What is it?," he asked, looking back and forth between it and Rebecca.

"I think it's a map, perhaps the gold," she said, trembling with excitement.

Jim's mind was racing, and he could barely listen as she explained how she came to have the parchment and how it made sense to her that it could be a map to the gold if it was in the pocket of a coat that may have been worn during the surrender. She admitted to Jim that it was a stretch, and there were lots of holes in the logic, but it made some sense, especially if there was any truth at all to the innkeeper's story.

"It's better than nothing, and better than stomping aimlessly around the forest," she said.

Jim asked if she was going to share this with Tom and fortune hunters.

"No!" she said.

Rebecca then told Jim she was angry at how the deal with the fortune hunters had been structured by Tom and offended that the tribe's cut had been so small, and she knew he had to be upset.

"I am, but I didn't know what to do," he said.

"Here's what we'll do," Rebecca said, "and now's the time. The fortune hunters are gone for a week.

"We'll use this map and find it ourselves. And you'll get it all!"

Chapter Thirty-Three

They arrived at one of the most remote gated entrances to the forest before dawn the next day with a low fog clinging to the ground, the trees and bushes dripping from the night's moisture, and the song birds greeting the sun as it began to rise.

Rebecca and Jim looked at each other, not sure where to begin.

He had stayed up all night with Rebecca's map and concluded it was basically useless. It was on a kind of parchment paper that was brittle and the writing on it, whatever it was, had faded. The actual markings, from what he could tell, appeared to be a rudimentary triangulation from some unknown starting points. He could make out a small "x" and the letters "113stps" and what appeared to be a circle or hump in the middle of the triangulation.

He compared the map to his own maps of the forest and tried to match what he saw on the parchment with what he saw on his maps and hope some magic would happen or lightning would strike and reveal a trend or a hint or a clue about where to start.

The only good clue was what appeared to be a squiggle on the map. It could be a stream, or it could be a crease in the parchment caused by the passage of time. He used a magnifying glass and concluded that it was most likely part of the drawing and not part of the parchment, so he concluded their focus should be on one of the seven or eight streams and tributaries that meander through his forest.

Good gracious, he thought. *I wonder if this is even worth it.*

But here they were, at the front gate to possibly an incredible future, and in their hands was either a piece of priceless history that would unlock unspeakable treasure or a piece of worthless parchment paper that would unlock nothing.

"I don't know," Rebecca said. "Let's just start walking along one stream after another and see if we can find a clue. Unless you have a better idea."

Jim, of course, didn't, and concluded in his mind that this was a pointless waste of time, except that spending the day walking along streams in his beloved forest wasn't all bad.

It's hard work to walk along streams. They twist and turn, and the ground in some places is eroded and drops steeply into the stream. There are trees, and tree roots, and stones that have to be negotiated, and briars and other entanglements that made the walk difficult. In some of the popular places, regular foot traffic had worn rough paths into the ground, but that's rare.

So, the walk was tough, and they needed to look around, heads up, for clues while they walked and not fall into a hole or into the stream.

With every step they took, the forest surrounding them with its trees and stones and streams could match the spot on the map. Or not match it at all.

By day four, their search had been predictably futile. All they'd found were some beer cans and the remnants of a couple of camp fires, and some stakes and other markings from the students who worked for the fortune hunters. They also pulled up all the survey stakes they could find, just to make a point.

As they walked through the forest, Jim tried to make sense of the limited clues on the parchment, clues the forest seemed unwilling to give up.

When they paused for a water break, Jim asked Rebecca to let him look at the map again.

He stared at it and turned it upside down hoping for a revelation. It wasn't clear which way was north and turning it didn't help much.

"What are you looking for?" Rebecca asked.

"I'm trying to figure out what that hump is," Jim said. "Maybe we're looking for the wrong thing."

"We don't know what we're looking for," she said with a shrug. "All we're doing is hoping to stumble into something that makes sense."

"This might be crazy, but something has just occurred to me," Jim said.

"Tell me," she said.

Chapter Thirty-Four

The university president sat alone in his luxurious office, awaiting the top of the hour when he would move to an ornate meeting room down the hall and face the school's board of trustees.

In academia, a leader can survive an occasional lapse of judgement or a bad outcome to a pretty good decision. If you're beloved and have built a bank of respect and admiration, you can dodge the assassins when they start circling to chop off your head. However, if the campus and community don't love, trust or respect you, your margin for error is very tiny.

And if you make the mistake of not promptly firing a losing football coach or prancing your naked ass in a porn video for all the world to see, there is no safety net.

So, this is where he was today.

He had ignored the advice of everyone around him and had filed a lawsuit against his fundraising lover, alleging that she was responsible for the embarrassing smut and that she was the one who had arranged for their gymnastics to be videotaped. His close circle of counselors argued strenuously and in vain that such a lawsuit would only bring more attention to the video and that the furor and laughter were dying down and why poke this dog with a stick, especially now.

The lawsuit was breaking news, naturally, and gave the TV stations another reason to rehash the story. Only fifteen minutes of the video had been distributed over the university email system, but a local TV reporter somehow mysteriously obtained the entire video and, during broadcasts over several days, had shown blurred-out excerpts to the TV station's audience. Ratings during that period had gone up fifteen percent as shocked and disgusted viewers couldn't take their eyes off the bedroom romp.

One of the campus fraternities obtained a complete version and posted it on their Facebook page with a humiliating count-down clock added to the screen that timed, from start to writhing, groaning finish, the university president's embarrassing brief time in the saddle, so to speak. After complaints from the university, the fraternity removed the post just before Facebook was going to pull the plug on it.

And then there was more salacious breaking news when the video appeared on a popular porn site as part of a compilation that included all the videos that had been taped from the bedroom lamp. The porn site named the compilation "Fundraiser has fun raising more than funds" and it quickly became one of the most viewed videos on the site, racking up more than one million views in the first week alone. He was a porn star, and the local TV news wouldn't shut up about it.

A local judge immediately tossed out his lawsuit against the fundraiser, declaring as preposterous the president's claim that his lover had arranged to record and circulate the nastiness because it would only serve to embarrass her and jeopardize her own career and expose her as a slutty hussy who was entertaining multiple gigolos in her apartment.

The wife of one of those gigolos, on a side note, filed for divorce, demanding that she be awarded everything she and her cheating husband had accumulated together. To the delight of the local TV stations, she provided more breaking news when she filed her own lawsuit, accusing the fundraiser of all sorts of things that contributed to the destruction of her marriage after her husband was videoed with the fundraiser enthusiastically bouncing on top of him, including alienation of affection and a charge of something called "criminal conversation," which is a lawyerly way of saying they had sex. The TV stations had even more fun when they followed a tip and discovered that the wife had moved out of the marital home and was now living with her girlfriend.

So, here sat the president, waiting for the

clock to strike the top of the hour and the ax to fall on his neck.

But his thoughts at the moment were not on the likely final moments of this career. He knew that his little shell company would probably be exposed. And why not? Everything else had gone to hell. He had looked at the contract with The Eno Club investors and was disgusted that his attorney hadn't included a non-refundable provision. What an idiot.

If they demanded a refund, which certainly seemed likely, he was screwed. The bank in Caymans provided absolute discretion and security for clients like his shell company, but the cost of those services was a requirement that the entirety of any deposit remain untouched for at least two years. So, he couldn't refund their money, at least for a while. He thought about what would happen if he simply disappeared, just evaporated where nobody could find him. But it would be two years before he could withdraw any of the money to live on.

He glanced at the clock and still had a few minutes.

He was grasping for options. One option

was to ask for, or demand, a severance from the university of say, three million dollars in cash and maybe a little bump in his retirement account. He briefly felt better as he developed a little plan in his head where his shell company would settle with The Eno Club for say, a million, because after all, he had provided some services to them that had value. If the trustees approved the cash severance, he could actually end up with four million and come away a winner. He smiled at this prospect.

But he needed a backup plan that he could execute quickly, as in the next few minutes. He pulled out some accounting papers showing the budgets and cash flows of the various university departments that reported to his office and several of the school's most well-funded endowments that threw off millions in interest income every year. He developed in his mind a scheme where he could quickly authorize and approve payments in small amounts from a variety of university accounts and endowments to his shell company, just enough to give him a million or so dollars so he could partially satisfy the investors.

He turned to his desktop and accessed his private documents where he kept copies of boilerplate invoices for the shell company. He knew all the information and codes the university required to process an invoice, so he rapidly created invoices to six different departments for research and consulting services, all in odd amounts that together added up to a million two hundred thousand. He printed the bogus invoices and approved them himself to avoid time-consuming scrutiny that would be required if the invoices were delivered to the departments and went through their approval process. He marked them "urgent" and put them in his out-box for his secretary to handle.

And, with that, it was time to go down the hall.

Chapter Thirty-Five

<hr>

Rebecca looked at Jim like he was crazy. *How can we possibly find a hump on the ground in a two-thousand-acre forest,* she asked herself.

Jim's theory made as much sense as anything, but it didn't seem possible that they could find it. After all, there must be hundreds or thousands of humps and swells throughout the forest. It would be a total miracle to find the right one, even if Jim was right.

Jim was trying to convince her that the odd marking on the parchment map that looked like a hump might be an Indian mound, where the natives buried their dead and usually included some of the deceased belongings like tools and arrows and clothing. They would pile rocks on top of everything, then cover it with dirt, hence the mounding effect. Hundreds of such mounds had been found in the surrounding counties, usually by farmers who were clearing timber to create fields. Some of them were quite large, and most farmers were respectful and would leave them undisturbed, which is why you would often see an odd stand of undisturbed trees in the middle of a tobacco field.

"I'm wondering," Jim said, "if they could've buried the gold in an Indian mound, perhaps near a stream. Could that be what the map is saying?"

Rebecca didn't know what to think anymore. It seemed like their secret treasure hunt was running out of ideas and time, with the real treasure hunters due to return in a couple of days.

The sun was beginning to set, and it would get dark quickly in the thick forest. It was a thirty-minute walk back to the gate, so they agreed they would follow one of the streams in that direction as far as they could, then jump on a trail where the walking would be easier and they would be out of the woods when it got dark.

They had already walked this stream once, going in the other direction, so they crossed to the other side for the walk out.

This is so beautiful, Rebecca thought. It's been worth all we've done even if we don't find the gold. The sun was setting ahead of them, sending soft shafts of light through breaks in the foliage, like spotlights on a Broadway stage, as the forest and its inhabitants began to settle for the night.

Suddenly, Jim stopped and thrust his hand in the air, like he was signaling for the cavalry behind him to come to a halt.

"What is it?" Rebecca said, immediately looking around for a snake or threatening varmint.

"Look up there," Jim said, pointing toward the setting sun.

"I don't see anything," she said.

"Come here," Jim said and pulled her arm so that she was standing next to him.

"Do you see it now?" he asked.

"Oh my god," Rebecca whispered, stunned.

There in front of them, and backlit by the setting sun, were two enormous oak trees, hundreds of feet tall. These were ancient trees, with trunks dozens of feet in diameter.

About seventy feet up, two of the largest limbs on each tree reached out to each other, and crossed, forming a rudimentary "x" along the rooftop of the forest.

Jim and Rebecca looked at each other, Rebecca at first thinking they were willing to see a clue anywhere, even in the sky or trees.

She didn't know whether to feel ashamed or hopeful or embarrassed or sad. Here they were, two virtual strangers in the middle of this forest, and their only clue was the crossed limbs of two oak trees. She closed her eyes and dropped her chin to her chest in resignation.

"Jim," she said with her eyes still closed. "This is ridiculous. There's no way those trees were like that a hundred and fifty years ago.

The trees may have been here, but surely their limbs weren't crossed, or at least not crossed enough for a soldier to use them as a reference point. I think we're grasping at straws here."

When she lifted her head and looked at Jim, he was looking at her as if she'd stabbed him the heart.

"This is something," he said quietly. "We have nothing else."

"Let's come right back here tomorrow," she said, shaking her head, "and see if this is anything at all. But this is pretty sketchy. Let's not waste much more time on it."

They returned to the large oaks just after dawn the next day. It was an overcast morning, with rain likely later in the day. The old trees looked different in the morning light, and their crossed limbs were less stark without the sun behind them, less enticing today as a place to start than they were yesterday.

They had a brief discussion about whether those limbs would've been crossed a hundred and sixty years ago when the map was drawn, and this issue was a reasonable dilemma until they remembered they had no other clues whatsoever.

Rebecca and Jim looked at the old map, which they had brought with them, and tried to get their bearings. They agreed that the writing on the map "113 stps" meant that the treasure was located one hundred thirteen steps from some point, probably from the base of one of the trees. So, for the rest of the morning in the dampness of the forest, they took pieces of string and paced off one hundred thirteen steps from the base of each of the giant oaks in twelve different directions and placed a stake in the ground at the end of each string. If viewed from above, their efforts looked like the face of a clock or a compass.

They were frustrated by the results.

There was nothing remarkable at the end of the strings, just the usual small trees and plants that were found throughout the forest. They walked around and around their string creation looking for any mounding or indentation, but there was nothing unusual about that area of the forest floor.

Jim proposed they dig holes in the areas where the strings ended, but they together concluded that was unproductive if there were no other clues.

Out of frustration, Jim got on his belly near the base of one of the oaks, down where the smell of the damp, rotting leaves was intoxicating if you loved the forest like him. He got as close to the ground as he could and slowly squirmed and shifted his view around the clock-like circle of string. He got as far as seven o'clock.

"There," he shouted to a startled Rebecca. "There' something!"

"What?" she asked, moving quickly to where he lay on his belly and dropping to the ground on her own belly.

"If you look from here, you can see a slight rise in the ground!"

He was pointing to a spot about twenty feet beyond their strings, and she saw it also.

They jumped up and brushed off the leaves from their bellies, moving quickly to the spot.

He used his shovel to rake away the pine straw and leaves from the little mound, and his shovel immediately hit a stone. And then another. The more debris he raked away, the more stones there were.

He stopped and looked at Rebecca.

"These stones shouldn't be here," he said. "They are quartz, and there's no quartz in this part of the forest, except maybe in creek beds. And there's no way there should be a pile of them here.

"They were brought from somewhere else. By a person."

Chapter Thirty-Six

The breaking news at noon was the retirement of the university president, and he was thanked for his service and all his contributions to the school, and the provost would be interim president while a national search was conducted for a replacement. Of course, it was another opportunity for the TV stations to speculate that the cause of his sudden retirement was his performance in the porn video.

The board of trustees meeting was brief and justice swift. He was fired for cause. The main reason was his sexual relationship with a subordinate employee, caught on tape for all to see so there was not much disputing those facts. His request for a large cash severance was denied, but he would be paid his normal salary for three years if he signed a document that he wouldn't sue the university for any reason or comment publicly on his dismissal. All activity in his office was ordered to be frozen, and the computers of his secretary and other administrative support staff were locked, and they were asked to leave for the day but assured that their jobs were not in jeopardy.

After he left the meeting, the board of trustees handled an additional piece of business. They approved a cash settlement with the president of Chi Omega, who was enraged when she learned that her lover was cheating on her. She was pre-law and pretty astute and recognized that he was weak and vulnerable, and she likely could benefit from his troubles. She easily found an attorney who gleefully filed a multimillion-dollar lawsuit against the university on her behalf, alleging that the president's entanglements with a student were a violation of the trust placed in him and. The lawsuit argued persuasively that she was entitled to be compensated for these violations, obviously ignoring the fact that she had a key to his office and was an enthusiastic participant in their assignations.

The board's final act of a busy day cleaning up messes was to direct the provost, who was now in charge, to make sure the deputy fundraiser got the boot, and they didn't care how it was handled as long as it didn't cost a lot and didn't result in a lawsuit.

Then they adjourned, wondering how it ever got to be like this.

The beleaguered ex-president had been ordered to leave campus immediately, and his belongings would be packed and sent to his home. He was filmed exiting the back of the building, the door held open by a security guard, by an enterprising tv reporter who had been tipped off.

What no one expected was that a former well-known basketball player would step from the bushes and create dramatic breaking news when he popped the president in the nose, shattering it in a bloody mess.

Chapter Thirty-Seven

Jim returned with a shovel. Rebecca had pulled away the leaves and some of the dirt with her hands, and there was a clear pattern to the stones, which were roughly lined up across the top of the slight mound.

Jim put the shovel on the side of the mound and placed his foot on the top of the blade, ready to push in, when he jumped back as if electrocuted, as if whatever was under these rocks and dirt had reached out of the ground and tried to strangle him.

"I can't do it," he gasped, anguish on his face.

Rebecca was startled.

"You can't do what?" she asked, moving to him and placing her hand on his shoulder.

"If this is a burial mound, my faith won't let me do this," he said.

"Tell me," she said impatiently.

"If this is an Indian burial mound," he explained, "we are taught as children that these are sacred sites, never to be disturbed. And to do so, to search for artifacts or whatever was buried with the deceased, would cause a scourge on us and our families and our homes. The spirit of the dead will follow us until we die and cause misery and heartache and illness."

"Give me the shovel," Rebecca said, anxious and excited to find what was in the mound.

She used the tool to push away the rocks on very top of the little mound and then shoveled away the dirt as fast as she could, anxious and excited to learn what they'd found. The work was difficult, and she wasn't accustomed to such manual labor, so her pace slowed quickly, and then she took a quick rest, leaning on the shovel.

After she caught her breath, she returned to the small hole she had dug into the top of the mound. She tossed away two or three small shovels of dirt, and then put her foot to the shovel to dig deeper.

The shovel hit something and stopped. She looked at Jim, and then pushed with all her remaining strength.

Because of the dirt, she couldn't see the tip of her shovel push through the rubber, causing a six-inch tear and releasing a ghastly stench that caused her to stumble backward, gasping and retching and gagging, finally falling to her hands and knees, vomiting on the side of their little mound.

"Oh no," Jim thought, "surely not." He pinched his nose as the smell hit him.

This is no Indian burial mound, he thought. *But I know what it is.*

He carefully took Rebecca's arm, helped her to her feet and to move away from the mound and its horror.

"It's the drug dealers or the mob," he said. "It's one of their victims."

Rebecca looked at him with shock, a dribble of vomit clinging to the corner of her mouth. It took her a minute to comprehend what Jim was telling her, then she began to remember the well-publicized and dramatic event when Jim fell in an old well that was filled with body bags.

"This must've been one of their early ones," he said, "before they started using the well."

As they sat there, they realized their search was in vain. Jim said they needed to call the sheriff and report the body.

When the fortune hunters returned from their train wreck experience, they found a section of the forest covered in a bizarre web of string and closed off with yellow police tape as the authorities conducted a perfunctory investigation that would eventually lead nowhere.

Chapter Thirty-Eight

fter three months, the search for the gold ended.

The fortune hunters had used every tool, trick and hunch in their arsenal to find it, and finally concluded that it either wasn't there or so well-hidden that nobody would ever find it. Rebecca had finally shared the parchment map, which they briefly thought would provide the necessary clue, but they finally concluded that the markings on the paper lacked any meaningful reference points and wasn't helpful at all.

So, no treasure for anyone.

The fortune hunters invested five million, and their gamble failed. They had gotten pretty creeped out anyway with the history of body bags and shootouts and questionable owner- ship. They furloughed the students who helped them, packed up their gear, and flipped off Tom as they left town. Tom called the Senator and told him the bad news, that the search had been called off. The Senator's first thought was that he'd been scammed in order to get the treaty ratified, but he knew Tom well enough to quickly push that thought from his mind. More or less.

Jim had planned to use the tribe's portion of the gold to pay for the construction of a small administration building and museum highlighting the history of the tribe. He even had picked out a spot for the building, near one of the main roads that went by the forest and overlooked one of the meandering streams.

Those plans would have to wait, but per- haps not for long.

With Rebecca's help, the tribe had negoti- ated an arrangement with the university so it could continue its ongoing research. It was a lucrative deal for the tribe and would provide a steady source of income for its small group of members. The university wanted a higher level of security to keep dead bodies from continuing to show up in the forest, so part of the negotiations was a contract to hire several of the tribe members to serve as a security detail and patrol the forest. Also, as part of the deal, Rebecca negotiated a requirement that the university fund the construction of a residential village to replace the rusted trailers and run-down shacks on Indian Road where the tribe now lived, including a connection to the local water and sewer system.

But that was all in the future.

All Jim had today was a new sign that had just been delivered and was laying on the ground. It was one of the proudest moments of his life.

He sat on his haunches and thought about all that had happened. He didn't understand everything, especially the experience in Washington, but he understood enough.

As his thoughts tumbled around in his head, he was happy and surprised to see Jezz emerge quietly from the forest with her arms outstretched, dressed in a magnificent leather outfit and her wild hair poofed up with more feathers than ever, a leather strap crossing her chest holding a canvas sack on her back. Jim was transfixed; he'd never seen her so glorious.

She glided toward her son, who stood up, and embraced him, and held him.

She looked at the sign and pointed to the post-hole digger.

"Generations have waited for this," she said quietly. "I'd like to share this moment with you."

He plunged his post-hole digger into the clay of his forest, digging a deep hole, and Jezz used a shovel to swirl some cement mix into the hole, and together they dropped in the pole supporting the sign. She tamped down the loose dirt with the shovel.

The sign read:

The Eno Club and Preserve
Proudly owned by the Oconeechee Tribe

JIM AND JEZZ held hands as they stood back and admired the sign, but only for a moment.

Jezz then twisted around and wriggled out of the strap that crossed her body, a strap that held the canvas knapsack. Jim could tell it was heavy, but his mother was a strong woman and effortlessly escaped the strap and dropped the knapsack on the ground between her and Jim.

"I've never known what to do with this," she said, pointing her toe at the knapsack. "And my father and his father didn't either. None of us ever knew who to trust or what would happen if someone knew.

"This has haunted me, and frightened me, and I couldn't wait to get it out of my house. And, today, you've brought me peace. Everything you've been through," she continued, tears in her eyes, "and everything you've done for this piece of earth, for our little tribe. You've proven yourself, and you've proven to me that you can figure out what to do with this."

Jim bent down, unfastened the knapsack's rusty buckles and pulled back the flap.

He'd never seen anything like what was inside.

He held the sack open with one hand and stuck the other inside to touch the brilliant gold pieces. He ran his hand through the gold, like he was sifting sand.

He looked up at his mother, who smiled.

"We've had it all along," she said. "For more than three lifetimes, our people were afraid of it, afraid that it would be taken from us, or used against us. And nobody had the courage or knowledge to turn it into something that could help us.

"You now have the courage. You'll know what to do."

His first thought was not to admit that he really did not know what to do, but he would never admit that to his mother, not in this moment.

So, he said nothing. He thought about the treasure hunters looking for something that could never be found, because it was under Jezz's bed or in her closet or wherever she'd hidden it for all her life. He thought all the hours he spent with Rebecca, gagging and retching on the damp forest floor, looking for a ghost, anxious to help him and his tribe, and to help herself as well.

He thought with sadness about how this bag of gold could've changed two or three generations of his people, lifting them from poverty and hopelessness, had any of them known what to do with it. He was frustrated, and almost angry, at the thought that the ramshackle neighborhood at the end of Indian Road could've been a place of pride and hope.

After a moment, he stood, his hand on the knapsack's strap.

Then, he pointed out to his mother that the tribe's name was misspelled on the sign.

"That'll have to be fixed," he said to her.

"Doesn't matter," she said warmly, "you've already fixed the hardest part."

Epilogue

Two soldiers returned from the neighboring farm with a stolen mule, the farmer's last item of any value and now the damned northern invaders had taken that also.

The mule was the last requirement needed by the newly promoted young captain to complete the orders issued by his general to provide payment to some Indians for services rendered during the war.

He already had the gold, issued from the army's bursar. It was in canvas sacks and only about half of what had been promised. The captain had substituted worthless confederate metal in some of the sacks and placed them in the bottom of the trunk that was to be delivered to the Indians. He placed sacks of gold on top of the fakes, and kept one for himself, storing it secretly in a satchel in his tent.

When he was ready, his soldiers loaded the trunk onto a small gun wagon and hitched it to the mule, and he sent for the Indians with word that their payment was ready.

He briefly felt guilty for cheating them because they had fought bravely and provided his general with valuable information that helped him plan an effective strategy against the confederates in this area. He thought about his West Point training and the values instilled at the military academy about honor and bravery and integrity. He truly believed in all that, but the war had hardened him, and he still had difficulty reconciling that some of the graduates of the same academy he attended had forsaken their commitments and their honor and their oaths when they led armies of rebels in an uprising against his nation.

The Indians had killed for the northern

cause, and some had been killed and probably deserved better than what they were receiving, but this was war.

When the Indian leader and two of his people arrived for their payment, they were dressed more like poor farmers in the area than natives, with dirty denim and cotton shirts and floppy hats. The lieutenant opened the trunk for their inspection, but they merely looked inside, shook their heads in agreement, took the reins of the mule, and walked away.

The captain had planned all along to follow them, so he told one of his sergeants that he would be on a mission the rest of the day and gave him some orders that would keep his men busy until he returned. He needed to know the destination of the gold.

He grabbed his carbine and some ammunition and began following the Indians as they slowly made their way from Bennitt's farm and headed north, into a thick forest.

They were easy to follow. The mule moved at its own pace, and the path they followed was a footpath not meant for carts, so there were tree roots and rocks and ditches that stalled the cart, stopping the mule in its tracks before it would strain and lean into its harness to move the heavy cart forward.

After about two hours, they emerged from the forest and turned west onto a well-used trading path which went from a train depot to the old colonial capital of Hillsboro. In sixty years or so, this trading path would be widened and smoothed to accommodate vehicles that the young captain couldn't imagine, but the curves would not be straightened nor would the hills be leveled, causing a new generation of travelers to wonder about the sanity of the road designer.

He turned west as well. The Indians walked so slow that it was difficult for him to match their pace and not catch them and overrun them. But he was careful.

After another hour, they approached the intersection where this trading path crossed a similar north-south path, and the Indians suddenly stopped and put their hands in the air. The captain quickly stepped into a thicket next to the path.

Two men stepped out of the woods next to the

cart with single-shot muskets pointed at the Indians. The captain peered at the situation through his single-lens telescope. The men appeared to be poorly dressed, probably just common bandits or desperate confederates on their way home from war and stealing anything they could along the way. They had no idea of the treasure in the trunk, and he would not let them have it, because he intended for it to be his one day.

The first shot of his carbine dropped one of the men instantly. He quickly fired again, hitting the second one in the gut. The captain ran toward the cart, and toward the Indians who were confused about the source of the shooting, and then more confused when a familiar face ran toward them.

The second thief was on the ground, groaning, and in no position to be a threat. The captain wondered if he should end the thief's misery, but he gave out a gasp and stopped moving, relieving the young officer of making that decision.

"There might be more," he said to the Indians. "We need to get out of here!"

He threw open the trunk, grabbed one of the bags, flung it toward the Indian leader and yelled at them to run, which they did. They would probably get robbed again, but he couldn't worry about that.

He threw the other sacks on the ground and slapped the mule on its rear. It looked over its shoulder, unsure what to do, so he slapped it again, and it began slowing moving down the path, surely to be captured by some lucky person who would feed it and put it to work again.

The captain realized he would probably soon be robbed, so he wrestled the heavy sacks into the woods where he found a pile of rocks next to a small stream. He pulled the smaller rocks aside and dug with his hands as far as he could. He shoved the sacks deep into the hole, covered it with dirt, and then replaced the stones on top.

He stood up, satisfied that he had hidden them well.

He then looked around for landmarks so he could return when it was safe and retrieve his treasure. Nothing was obvious, so he returned to the trading path.

The captain stepped off the distance from where he stood to the intersection with the north-south trading path. He removed a small piece of parchment from his waist band and, with a piece of charcoal, marked the intersection with an "x" and noted the distance from that point to where he left the path to bury the gold.

113 stps

The young captain folded the paper, slipped it into the breast pocket of his uniform, and began the walk back to his army, to the momentous events that would occur in a few days at Mr. Bennitt's farm, and to a life that would always be comfortable because of what he'd just hidden in a pile of rocks. He would return for it one day and live in luxury forever.

The brown-skinned teenaged boy who had been watching everything remained in his hiding place in the tangled brush and didn't move, even when ants crawled over his feet and hands, and even when a black snake slithered closely by. He hated snakes. He waited for hours, until it was almost dusk, before he crawled from his hiding place.

The boy could carry only one of the sacks.

He left the others in the rock pile and disappeared into the brush, sliding effortlessly through the undergrowth toward a village in the woods where his family waited, hoping their son would return with a squirrel or a rabbit for their evening meal, only to be disappointed.

THE END

Afterglow

This was his favorite bar in the southern Caribbean, with a view overlooking the tiny harbor of Jost Van Dyke, a view today slightly tainted by the arrival of a small cruise ship, which cluttered things a bit but would sail away before he finished his third drink.

This bar was the ugly step-cousin to the more famous bar next door, which is actually a tourist trap and gift shop that happens to include a bar, the legendary Soggy Dollar. Cruise ship passengers disgorge almost daily from their floating palaces to ride rickety pickup trucks from the harbor, sit on the beach, and drink the famous Painkiller, a coconut rum concoction quickly slurped down by light-weight, amateur drinkers who ended up barfing in the warm sand next to their lounge chairs.

The tourists rarely make it past the Soggy Dollar to find his spot, Seddy's One Love Bar and Grill, so it was always cool and comfort-able and where locals spent their time.

This was one of his final evenings at the One Love before he loaded provisions on his boat and began the trek north as the Car-ibbean winter came to an end. His boat was moored off shore, and he could see it from his seat at the bar, gently rocking with its bow pointing into a breath of a breeze.

The MV Afterglow was too much boat for one person, but he had tried every other arrangement and his life was better when he was alone. At eighty feet, his four-million-dollar Johnson Flybridge was no problem to sail in calm, open waters by himself, but he had to radio for assistance from the local dockmaster when he was docking, and there were always a couple of guys eager to tie her up in exchange for a twenty-dollar bill.

Over the years, he'd hired guys to be deck hands and bosuns mates, most of whom were unreliable drunks. He'd also tried girls as cooks and deck hands, and they were too restless to last for long but surely made the nights more enjoyable.

In a few days, or maybe tomorrow (such was life on a boat), he would begin motoring north through the islands and toward Martinique. It was there that he would meet up with other cruisers like him, captains who preferred to operate their boats themselves and with no or minimal professional crew members. These captains would assemble into a small, loosely organized flotilla, and sail together toward Miami.

There is strength in numbers, especially in the open ocean, and they had done this together many times. It was reassuring to know that a fellow captain and his yacht were nearby if you had an engine problem or developed a navigational issue or ran out of beer.

These crossings between the islands and

mainland US were typically uneventful, except for occasional brutal and windy storms that tossed the mega yachts around like tin cans in a flooded river. The storms always came at night, it seemed, dousing the boats in sea water. But an experienced captain could manage unless his engines died, and then he was at the mercy of a merciless ocean until one of his buddies attached a tow line, a dangerous endeavor that usually required multiple attempts to be successful in a blustery storm.

His mind wandered as he drank his second drink of the evening at the One Love, watching with relief as the cruise ship in the harbor silently slipped away.

Now, he was thinking of the next voyage and whether to include her.

She was the One Love's afternoon and early evening bartender, which was when he typically was there. He wasn't a late-night guy at this point in his life.

She was stunning, with bright eyes and blond hair in Caribbean cornrows. She wore great earrings and necklaces, which was a spectacular look, and made him smile everyday with lively stories about being a bartender around the various islands. She was American, and college educated, but didn't talk much about that.

There was a sadness about her, though, and it took months of casual bar talk and growing familiarity for her finally to tell him about her life. And, of course, it involved a guy.

She'd gotten tangled up with him in Barbados, where she was tending bar and he was trying to make it taking tourists on fishing charters around the Caribbean. He was American also and had this complicated scheme where he leased fishing boats from their owners, operated them himself, and his clients were hand-me-down tourists who waited too late to make a reservation with a legitimate charter and figured a day on his boat was better than a day shopping with the wife.

He owned nothing, his crew was whoever was unemployed and at the dock the morning of a charter, and his rates were a deal because he didn't have any insurance or licenses.

She was more or less satisfied until they moved to Jost, where he found an additional niche hauling cocaine on the boats he leased from other people. She was completely opposed, but this segment of his business grew quickly, and he became a major deal in the southern islands. He became intoxicated with the big money and less and less tolerant of her complaining.

She knew in her heart that this was a world no one could escape. She was now trapped in a drug world where she knew too many details.

But she would leave if she could.

He listened to her story over several afternoons and evenings. It terrified him to learn any of this, and he instantly regretted probing her for details because he didn't want to be involved at all in any drug stuff. Yet, now he was in.

He decided he would offer her a way out.

And she said yes.

The plan he outlined was simple, but also complex, and ready to implement as soon as the time was right.

The next evening at the bar, she told the Afterglow skipper that her boyfriend definitely had a charter the next day and that his boat would leave the dock at six in the morning. The skipper gave her some very specific instructions to follow before she left the house for good.

At eight the next morning, he also was at the dock, waiting for her.

He made her promise that she would tell no one where she was going, or that she even was leaving by sea or on a yacht and certainly not the name of the boat. Say nothing. She could call the bar from the boat and quit over the phone. He assured her money was no problem, so forget about her last check.

The Afterglow was too big for the little dock at Jost, so he brought the Afterglow's dingy to pick her up. The dingy was painted with the Afterglow's name, so he taped over the name and registration number just to be safe. He wasn't sure what he'd do if someone followed them, or watched them from shore, but he had a plan for that. Sort of.

She finally arrived in a junk island cab. She had two large suit cases, and it was going to push the dingy to handle the bags and both of them, but he'd make it work, he hoped.

He loaded her and her stuff into the dingy,

and as they sat down to push away from the dock, she quickly kissed him on the cheek and said thank you.

The dingy puttered out of the quiet little dock and out into the bigger harbor. In case anyone was watching, he went first to a large four-mast sailing yacht, and went around it, so the sailing boat blocked the view of the dingy from shore and perhaps trick a spy into thinking that the sailing yacht was the dingy's destination. He then guided the dingy past his own boat, finally making a U-turn and tying up at the stern of the Afterglow.

As soon as they were aboard, he used the boat's hydraulic lift to return the dingy to its berth, cranked the twin diesels, lifted the anchor, and made way for anywhere but here.

He decided to put as much distance as possible between them and her boyfriend, so they cruised for almost thirty-six hours before stopping except for one break for fuel. He made her comfortable in her own cabin, and she slept through the night as he manned the bridge.

After that marathon, they would sail for partial days and stop early enough to enjoy a swim before making their way ashore to the nearest waterfront bar for drinks and food. She was great fun to be with. The sleep obviously helped, and he watched her face relax as the stress of her former life began to fade away. Their days and evenings were happy, filled with laughter and funny stories.

They were having great fun, but she showed no interest in a physical relationship or joining him in his cabin, and he was okay with that for now because he didn't want to come across as a creep or too pushy. The physical stuff would happen if it was meant to be, and if he was lucky.

They loaded the boat with provisions in Martinique and coordinated with their friends for the run through the upper Caribbean, the Tucks and Caicos and the fringes of the Bahamas to south Florida.

She admitted she was nervous about the long voyage because she didn't like rough seas, but he assured her that this time of year would be smooth and no chance of hurricanes.

The little flotilla consisted of six boats, most in the sixty-to-eighty-foot range, and one fifty-six- foot Sea Ray whose owner had met the others at a bar while they discussed the trip and begged to be included. He'd never made the trip before and admitted that he'd feel more comfortable in the company of an experienced group.

It was an hour before sunrise of the voyage's first night, and it had been a sleepless night ahead because of unexpected rough seas southwest of the Turks and Caicos. The Afterglow had tossed and groaned all night, but her twin diesels kept humming as she thumped and wallowed through the rolling seas.

The flotilla wasn't exactly a military operation, so the boats were scattered about in a loose formation that was hardly a formation at all. But they usually were within sight of each other's bobbing navigation lights, always could see each other on their sophisticated radars, and were constantly jabbering on the marine radios just to keep everyone awake. On this early morning, the rough seas had slowed the smaller Sea Ray, and he had fallen about five miles behind the rest.

Suddenly, the radio on every boat erupted.

"Mayday, I'm being attacked!"

None of the captains had ever heard an actual mayday call.

It was the captain of the Sea Ray, and he sounded frantic.

"A speedboat has come up fast from behind, and he's right on my stern," the radio blared. "I spotlighted him, and he has a gun!"

The Afterglow captain answered quickly.

"Full throttles, a zig zag route. Maybe your wake will slow him down. We're on our way! Shoot a flare so we can find you! Let's go guys!"

All five of the big cruisers quickly began to turn toward the southeast, hoping to soon spot their beleaguered friend. The Afterglow captain's mind was racing, wondering how this guy came up on them so fast and didn't show up on their radar.

"Shots fired," came the next cry on the radio.

"We're on our way, ten minutes," replied the Afterglow.

The Afterglow captain peered through the darkness and could see the Sea Ray's navigation lights ahead. He could clearly see the two boats on his radar. The boats seemed to be together and spinning in a circle.

He radioed his buddies to turn on all their spotlights, hoping the show of strength would frighten off whomever was bothering the Sea Ray.

"He's trying to come aboard! He's a fucking pirate!" shrieked the radio.

The Afterglow throttled back as it approached the two boats, and its captain could now see a sleek speedboat with one person on board, rocking in the heavy seas next to the Sea Ray.

"What's going on?" the Afterglow radioed to his fellow captain.

"He wants a girl! He's demanding to know where a girl is!" the Sea Ray said on the radio. "I told him we don't have any girls!

"Now he's dead in the water. He's not moving. He can't get away!"

The captain suddenly realized that this was no pirate, but a kidnapper, probably sent by the drug hauler boyfriend. He had attacked the right flotilla but the wrong boat. How did he know where they were?

The girl emerged from the cabin where she was sleeping, hair tousled, eyes heavy, wanting to know what's going on.

"Go back inside, now!" he yelled to her.

By now, the other cruisers had arrived and encircled the confusing scene. Their blinding spotlights clearly showed a single person in the speedboat, which was tossing violently, with an occasional wave banging the speedboat into the side of the Sea Ray.

The kidnapper could barely stand up in his stricken boat as it rocked. He had both hands in the air as if to surrender but was holding what appeared to be an automatic rifle in one hand.

The Afterglow was the closest, so its captain got on its loudspeaker.

"Drop the weapon!"

The kidnapper ignored the demand. *May not speak English*, thought the Afterglow captain.

As the Afterglow rolled in the sea, its captain quickly stepped to his weapons locker which was behind a discreet, unmarked door on the bridge. He removed the AR-15, which had never been used, and slapped an ammunition clip into it, unsure whether the aged ammo would actually fire.

A shot across the bow is the international mariner's signal to stop and surrender, but he couldn't fire across the kidnapper's bow because the pirate was too close to the Sea Ray. So, he pointed the gun in the air and fired it three times in quick succession.

The kidnapper lowered his rifle, pointed it at the Afterglow, and let off a blitz of automatic fire.

The Afterglow captain had never been shot at in his life, so he didn't know what to do for a second. Then his instincts kicked in and he took aim at the kidnapper as best he could, but his boat and the speedboat were rocking so violently it was impossible to aim.

He switched the weapon to automatic and emptied the magazine in the direction of the speedboat.

The kidnapper disappeared from sight. *Surely, I hit him with something*, thought the Afterglow captain.

"Can you see into his boat?" he radioed to the Sea Ray.

"Yes," came the reply, "he's down, but alive. He's holding up a hand, like he's begging us to stop."

The first instinct of the Afterglow captain was to signal the flotilla to resume its journey and leave the injured kidnapper to suffer in his disabled boat in the middle of the ocean.

But he was pissed. This guy was a kidnapper, a modern-day pirate, and had fired a gun at him. He wasn't at all sure whether the Afterglow was damaged, but she seemed to be operating okay and he'd wait for sunrise to do a thorough inspection.

"Everybody move away from the speedboat," he said calmly into the radio, and the other boats angled away.

"If everybody is okay dealing with this guy in a permanent way, flash your lights," he said, as the lights of all the boats went off, then on. "Flash again if you agree to never speak of this to anyone." The lights all flashed.

He turned his attention back to the speedboat, where the kidnapper had struggled to his knees and was holding both hands out in front of him, as if pleading to not abandon him in this dire situation.

The Afterglow captain slapped another clip into the AR-15 and took aim.

He raked the speedboat from bow to stern. During the assault, the kidnapper disappeared, either shot or hiding.

Suddenly, a rogue wave hit the side of the stalled speedboat, and rolled it over, spilling its contents and the kidnapper into the sea. He had one hand in the air when he slid out of sight.

The Afterglow captain could see immediately what had disabled the speedboat. A half-inch line, perhaps from the Sea Ray, had become entangled in the starboard propeller, and tightened itself impossibly around the prop and drive shaft, even bending the supports that attached the equipment to the hull of the boat.

As the speedboat wallowed on its back, the Afterglow captain went to his weapons locker and returned to the bridge with his four-gauge shotgun, a gun so powerful and with such a recoil that he had to attach a cradle to the bridge's railing to make sure he didn't dislocate his shoulder shooting it.

Again, it was impossible to aim in these rough seas, so it took eight shots from the massive gun to open gaping holes in the speedboat's fiberglass hull, just at the waterline. Sea water flooded into the holes, and the speedboat quickly sank, stern first, with its bow pointing straight in the air as the sea swallowed it.

"We must never speak of this," the Afterglow captain said on the radio. "Now let's move on."

The rest of the trip was smooth and uneventful. He didn't tell her that the speedboat was there for her, and she didn't ask.

They were weary when they arrived at a yacht club in Palm Beach where he'd decided to dock for a few days to rest instead of his usual destination in Miami, a paranoid change of plans.

They enjoyed a lively couple of days in the Palm Beach social world and didn't rest a bit. They went shopping to get her some clothes that were more appropriate for the yachting world, including some bathing suits he couldn't wait to see her in.

They continued their trip with an idyllic cruise up the Intracoastal Waterway, with smooth and easy sailing, lots of places for fuel, and great waterfront restaurants, most of which had docks large enough for the After-glow and waiters who were happy to help tie her up for a couple of twenties.

About midway through Florida, they were stopped by the US Coast Guard, which de-manded to be allowed to board the Afterglow.

Permission was granted, of course, and the Coast Guard said they were checking many of the large yachts that had recently come north from the islands because of rumors they were loaded with cocaine for the addicts in the big cities of America. Their search was thorough, and the drug-sniffing dog found nothing.

"What's this?" asked one of the heavily armed sailors.

He pulled a pen from his pocket and bent over, sticking the end of the pen into the opening of a spent AR-15 shell casing which had been hiding under the deck rail all this time.

"Weapons check at sea, sir," replied the Afterglow captain, relieved that the sailor handed him the shell.

The Coast Guard thanked them, returned to their patrol boat, and the Afterglow resumed its northward crawl.

She wanted to know their plan. It was the first time she had been interested in where they were going since they'd departed Jost Van Dyke.

He told her they would spend two or three weeks at a place called Hilton Head, an island in South Carolina where there was a wonderful tiny harbor, lots of nightlife and great restaurants, and a world-class golf course that was the site of a professional golf tournament that would be played while they were there. He described the scene at the harbor with the lively crowds and excitement, and she seemed interested. This was an annual tradition for him, and he loved it. He hoped she would, also.

They arrived at Hilton Head late one afternoon and sailed in slow circles in the Calibogue

Sound while he talked on the radio with the dockmaster. The Afterglow had a dock reservation, but there was a mix up and the large berth the boat required was blocked by some little boat, and they couldn't find its owner so the dockmaster and his crew were untying it themselves, unhooking the electricity and water lines, and pulling it to an adjacent dock to make room.

He always had the same berth, which was adjacent to a busy sidewalk, and it was one of the few that could accommodate the Afterglow. He had learned over the years that it was also easier to back the Afterglow into the harbor through the narrow entrance rather than enter bow first and then have to turn the boat around in the tight harbor. It was nerve-wracking to enter harbor entrance because a crowd always gathered at the narrow entrance to watch the big boats glide past, pointing and wagering on whether they'd bump into something.

Together with the staff of the dockmaster, they secured the Afterglow and went to the tiny nearby grocery for essentials, then headed out for a walking tour of the harbor area.

She loved it and laughed and nearly pranced as they walked around. It was a perfect evening, except for a local specialty called no-see-ums, tiny almost invisible bug devils that swarm your face, get in your hair and nose, and make you itch like crazy. They dashed back to the grocery for bug spray.

They had wonderful days. They bought passes to the golf tournament and followed some of the famous golfers, even though she'd never heard of most of them, but the setting was so beautiful and relaxing that just walking around was a pleasure. On the final day of the golf tournament, a Sunday afternoon, the tournament was coming to its conclusion, and they watched from a grandstand as the players tackled the eighteenth and final hole, a picturesque spot overlooking the harbor, of which the Afterglow was a prominent feature. He could see his boat from the grandstand, and was proud, especially when he saw passersby stopping to point and admire it.

When the golf tournament ended, they slowly walked with the big crowd back to the harbor and to have a cocktail on the stern of the Afterglow and watch the people go by.

As they approached the Afterglow, she grabbed his arm, grabbed it so hard that it hurt.

He stopped and turned and looked at her. Her other hand was over her mouth, eyes wide open in horror, her face the color of death.

"What on earth," he said. "Are you okay?"

"It's him," she said.

"Who? Where?"

She stepped behind him and pointed over his shoulder to the Afterglow, to two men standing in the lounge area on its stern.

"Is that him?" he asked.

"My boyfriend," she said in a quivering voice. "I don't know the other guy."

He knew this day would come, and that it might be today, so he was ready and unsurprised. He pulled her out of the foot traffic and partially hid behind a bush next to the walkway. She was sobbing.

He looked at the two men on his boat. The boyfriend looked normal, but the other guy looked fearsome, like a mobster or enforcer or fixer or something. The captain smiled ever so slightly when he saw the boyfriend's hat.

He told her to stay right here.

He walked toward his boat. He felt safe, at the moment. There were too many people milling around for something bad to happen.

"Can I help you?" he asked them when he arrived at his boat and stepped on the small landing at the stern. "This is my boat."

"Where is she?" the boyfriend said firmly.

"Who?" the captain said.

"You know who. Where is she?"

The captain thought for a minute.

"You have five seconds to get off this boat," he said.

The two men didn't move.

"You're in violation of maritime law by being here," he said, just as firmly, and making stuff up as he went along. "The Coast Guard is out in the sound and can be here within minutes. And there are cops everywhere. Now, get off this boat!"

"We're not leaving without her," the boyfriend said, and his buddy took a menacing half step toward the captain.

"Actually," the boyfriend continued, "we might leave without her."

His buddy pulled back his jacket to show a pistol in his waistband, just like on TV.

"And we might take this boat, and you, and deal with you and still find her later. Is that what you want?"

The captain couldn't believe these threats were being uttered with other boats docked on either side of him and happy tourists and golf fans walking just a few feet away.

"How'd you find me?" came the voice behind him. She had emerged from hiding and stood on the sidewalk, glaring at her boyfriend.

"Come on the boat," the boyfriend said. "Let's talk."

"I'll talk right here," she said. "How'd you find me?"

"I'm not gonna yell back and forth with you. Come on board and let's talk," said the boyfriend.

She looked at the captain, who gently nodded, and stepped aboard.

They all went inside the main cabin and shut the sliding glass doors.

"How'd you find me?" she asked in a low growl, leaning forward as if to pounce.

"I've been tracking you since you left the house, you dumb bitch," said the boyfriend with a sneer.

The Afterglow captain had to stifle a laugh as he marveled at the irony of what he just heard.

That's because the Afterglow had not always been the Afterglow.

At one time, it was the Moonbeam.

It was built and proudly owned by an attorney who scored big in the enormous tobacco lawsuit settlement in the late nineties in which he had represented some successful plaintiffs. His share of the settlement was breathtaking, and he bought every toy imaginable, including the Moonbeam. Along the way, he developed a healthy appetite for coke, and then he developed an even greater appetite for importing the stuff. The money was great, but the thrill was even greater.

His scheme was to use the Moonbeam to pick up loads of cocaine off the coast of North Carolina, a ton at a time packaged in fifty-pound increments. He and the Moonbeam would meet a smuggler in open seas just over the horizon from the coast and bring the stuff into the Cape Fear River, offloading it to small fishing boats at the docks at Southport or Bald Head Island. He would always fill the Moonbeam with diesel at the docks, which could be as much as three thousand dollars, a big sale that would ensure that the nosy dockmasters would ignore the shady transfer of packages at their fuel dock.

He and the Moonbeam became an essential link in the coke smuggling business in that part of the world. Then he got greedy.

The lawyer decided to cut out the middle man, the guys in the fishing boats who took the coke to backwater docks where it was loaded on trucks for delivery to the dealers in Fayetteville, Charlotte and Raleigh. His big plan was to forget those guys and take the Moonbeam all the way up the river just past Wilmington to a defunct dock and warehouse he leased and where he would transfer the load directly to the delivery trucks, thus preserving for himself the cut of the action that went to the fishermen.

They, of course, were pissed.

He arrived at the defunct dock on his inaugural run with a ton and a half of pure coke in the belly of the Moonbeam, five trucks lined up on the dock to take the load.

The bust was over in minutes. The feds, tipped off by the pissed fishermen, emerged from everywhere, the back of the trucks, decrepit boats moored nearby, bushes along the river, and from a helicopter that noisily swept in.

The lawyer went to prison forever, and the Moonbeam was confiscated and became the property of the DEA. It was towed to a nearby boat yard, where it would be moored and maintained until the DEA could dispose of it.

Before he retired, the Afterglow captain was the faceless bureaucrat at the DEA who made a career managing a team of other bureaucrats who disposed of assets confiscated in drug busts. It was a lucrative part of the government's business. Every year they sold or auctioned hundreds of millions of dollars' worth of airplanes, boats, thousands of cars, houses and farms. They also handled all the cash that was captured in the busts. They didn't get drugs; those were destroyed after the trials.

He worked on his retirement plan for several years and perfected a system to make confiscated assets simply disappear from the DEA's computer manifest. He could make it look like they never existed. He tested his system on small amounts of cash, and it worked perfectly. He then made a confiscated Mercedes disappear from the files, and reappear in his driveway with its title in his name.

As he prepared to walk out the door into retirement, he waved his magic wand over a large amount of cash and a yacht called the Moonbeam, which he had only seen in photos and would later transform into the Afterglow, and a suitcase full of DEA tricks and toys that might come in useful one day.

There was a minor dustup when one of his DEA colleagues, a front-line enforcement agent, figured out at the last minute that something was up when he couldn't locate an asset he needed for a long-delayed trial. His concerns were resolved when a captured Ferrari ended up free and clear in his garage. "The car's great," he told the captain, "and I won't talk, but you owe me."

So, now the captain stood in the main cabin of a yacht that wasn't technically his, with one of the Caribbean's largest coke smugglers, someone who appeared to be a hired killer, and a girl he barely knew whose life he was trying to save.

"Yeah," the boyfriend said smugly, "there's a bug in your suit case.

"We've been following you ever since you left," he continued, "and that's how we found you out of Martinique, and by the way, I haven't heard from my friend since. Maybe you can tell me what happened to him. You were moving every day, so we just waited until it looked like you had stopped for a while.

"So now you can come back with me and keep your mouth shut, or not," the boyfriend said menacingly, slightly motioning his head toward his buddy.

The captain had to suppress another smile as he looked again at the boyfriend's hat.

You've been tracking her, and I've been tracking you, you bastard, and I knew exactly when you'd get here.

Among the instructions he gave the girl before they departed Jost Van Dyke was to identify an item the boyfriend always had with him. She said it was his nasty fishing hat, wore it everywhere. He gave her a very thin silver wafer, the size of a quarter, one of the DEA's spy toys in the bag of tricks he'd taken and told her to put it in this headband of his hat before she left.

The captain had tracked this guy on his laptop and watched him come and go on a couple of fishing trips or drug hauls, before he watched him move north, only losing track of him while he was apparently on commercial airline flights. He was actually pleased that he showed when he did, because the battery in the wafer would give out in a few days.

When he saw on his laptop that the boyfriend was heading in their direction, he thought about what he would do and how he could ensure that he and the girl would be safe, not just today, but could escape this drug mess with their lives.

He had a plan, and now it was time to implement.

Before he approached his boat and confronted the boyfriend and his buddy, he used his mobile phone to send a three-digit code by text message, and received this message in return: "19:00, heading 023, 12 knts. 3 clicks when ready."

It was now fifteen minutes to seven, and the boyfriend growled, "Let's go," and the bad guy showed his gun again.

The captain gave a reassuring look to the girl, who didn't appear very reassured, and moved efficiently to prepare the Afterglow for departure. When he was ready, he cranked the engines and let them warm for a moment before the girl released the lines holding them to the dock.

It was exactly seven o'clock when the Afterglow smoothly left its berth and slid through the narrow harbor entrance, a nice crowd on the sidewalks waving happily to the handsome boat, unaware of the crisis on board.

The sun was setting beautifully over the sound as the captain pushed the throttles ahead and settled the Afterglow at twelve knots and a southwesterly course.

He looked over his right shoulder and saw an offshore fishing boat, about two hundred yards away, moving a little faster than him but on the same course.

He pushed the thumb key on his marine radio three times: *click, click, click.*

A response was immediate. *Click, click, click.*

He glanced to the rear upper deck of his boat where his three passengers were gathered. And he jammed the throttles of the Afterglow as far as they would go.

The big boat leapt forward, diesels shrieking, bow soaring into the air, stern down as her pair of five-bladed screws dug into the salt water.

The thug was leaning on a deck rail, and the sudden surge sent him overboard. The boyfriend lost his footing and slid on his butt into the rear deck panel, unable to regain his footing with the deck at a crazy angle. The girl slid into him, further hindering his recovery, and then smacked him in the head with an oar.

The captain quickly pulled the throttles to idle as two heavily armed DEA agents sprung from their hiding places in the Afterglow's forward heads. The offshore fishing boat swung violently toward them and quickly pulled aside, launching other agents onto the Afterglow. Some of them fished the thug out of the drink.

It was over in about a minute.

The DEA was thrilled, with high fives all around on the deck of the Afterglow because they really wanted the boyfriend but couldn't catch him unless he stepped on US soil, and now they had him thanks to a nifty trap set by one of their former colleagues.

The Afterglow captain pulled aside the DEA team leader.

"Even?" he asked the Ferrari owner.

"Even."

The DEA team took its trophies and departed as suddenly as it arrived, leaving only the captain and the girl and the Afterglow, and a tranquility that was a startling but welcomed contrast to the chaos of a few minutes earlier.

They returned to the dock, much to the delight of the sidewalk crowd who enjoyed watching the big boats move around.

Once the Afterglow was tucked in, she came to him.

"You saved my life," she said. "I was trapped. I was afraid to go home, afraid that he'd follow me and kill me and my family. You've set me free, and now I want to go home. I hope you understand."

So, she went home, and he was alone again on the Afterglow. His life was better when he was alone, he thought. No drama.

Two days later, he was having a drink at the Quartermaster, a great little bar that adjoins the dockmaster's office.

She was a really cute waitress with a warm, wonderful Southern drawl. She confided she was bored with this gig and her husband and was ready for change and excitement.

And now he was thinking of the next voyage.

THE END

My faithful readers – both of them – will hopefully recognize and remember portions of The Eno Club as a short story I wrote several years ago called "The Forest," which appeared in my short story collection "Vanessa." "The Forest" was always intended to be a longer and more involved story, but I never figured it out until it became a part of this novel. Perhaps I still haven't, but it made sense to me, and I hope to you as well.

Also, The Eno Club is a novel. It is not historical fiction. It is complete fiction. No time was spent on research, and I had fun fabricating absolutely everything.

As always, I am grateful to my favorite editor Lisa Piercy, who is always honest and helpful about my writing and provides valuable insights especially when my stories make no sense whatsoever.

I'm also indebted to Ashley Campbell and Nate McHenry for reading early versions of this mess and offering feedback and suggestions that dramatically improved the story.

Gene Upchurch is a native of Durham and a graduate of the University of North Carolina at Chapel Hill.

He was a sportswriter before embarking on a 28-year career in public affairs, community relations, and legislative advocacy in the utility industry. He is a proud recipient of the Order of the Long Leaf Pine, the State of North Carolina's highest civilian honor.

He lives in Pinehurst with this wife, Lisa, and their two Norwich Terriers, Shelby and Hootie.